MORE LADIES OF LETTERS

MORE LADIES
OF LETTERS

Carole Hayman and Lou Wakefield

CHIVERS LARGE PRINT
BATH

British Library Cataloguing in Publication data available

This Large Print edition published by Chivers Press, Bath, 2001.

Published by arrangement with Granada Media Ltd.

U.K. Hardcover ISBN0 7540 4491 2
U.K. Softcover   ISBN0 7540 4492 0

Printed and bound in Great Britain by
Bookcraft, Midsomer Norton, Somerset

Marbella University

Ten years ago my friends, Carole Hayman and Lou Wakefield, were kind enough to send me a batch of letters they had found in the drawer of a melamine cabinet at a boot fair in Kent.

These letters were part of a correspondence between a Mrs Irene Spencer and a Mrs Vera Small, women in their early sixties, and recorded the beginning of their friendship.

At that time my collection of historical documents was relatively small and had not yet become the all-embracing passion of my life. However, I recognised that the Spencer/Small Letters, (as they have since become known), were, potentially, extremely valuable, both in literary and financial terms. Few collectors at the time were interested in English domestic correspondence; especially that written by older women. Now, of course, with the widespread use of electronic communication devices, letters of any type have become extremely rare. When not on loan to University libraries and museums my Spencer/ Small letters are kept in a vault at Coutts, together with other rare collectable documents.

Imagine my delight and surprise last year

when a courier interrupted my study of a Sir Cliff Richard letter (to a fisherman pal on the Algarve) and handed me a large jiffy bag which bulged with yet more Spencer/Small letters! I was suspicious at first; there are many forgeries on the market. A period of rigorous investigation followed. I am particularly grateful to Professor Okawa of Nagasaki University for his invaluable work on 'the use of the ironic single quote in the letters of Vera Small'. This work helped to verify the letters. As did the work of Dr Karen Pigg of De Montfort University, whose dissertation, 'the later poetry of Irene Spencer—the voice of exile' provided me with yet more evidence that this latest batch of letters was indeed genuine. I will be forever grateful to the anonymous person who sent me these letters.

Because I was frantically busy with my new book, 'Ted Hughes—collected notes to the milkman' I asked Ms Wakefield and Ms Hayman to edit these latest Small/Spencer letters. They proved to be extremely sensitive editors. All libellous and unnecessarily cruel statements made by Irene and Vera about myself and my so called 'exploitation of private papers' have been removed, as have frequent libellous references to senior members of the Royal Family.

More Ladies of Letters provides us with an invaluable insight into the mindset of the contemporary British pensioner. The book

2

raises many questions: did the feminist movement [The advocacy of women's rights on the ground of the equality of the sexes] concentrate too much on the bra and neglect the support hose? Has Irene and Vera's heavy use of saturated fats over the years contributed to the dysfunctionalisation of their respective families? The renowned sexologist, Dr Marcus Cox, wrote in *Sexology Today* (Jan 5 1999), 'After reading the Spencer/Small letters I had to re-evaluate my life's work regarding the sexual appetite of the older woman.'

More Ladies of Letters is, however, very accessible and will appeal to the common reader. It is not only an historical document, it is a fascinating glimpse into the private worlds of two extraordinarily ordinary English women.

Sue Townsend
2000

Dear Vera,

DO NOT TEAR THIS UP. Read it first and then decide.

You will no doubt be surprised that I am writing to you after we both vowed never to communicate with each other again after the disastrous 'holiday' together last year. However a certain event has taken place which I feel duty bound to inform you of. I have tussled with my conscience as to whether to keep my distance and keep mum, but I find I cannot lie, not even (as politicians seem to do) by emission.

There is no nice way to impart the dreadful news I have to tell you. Bill Snapes is dead. You remember, of course, after dallying with us both, he set up with a girl half his age, and I think I told you they'd had a baby. I seem to recall us enjoying the joke of him having to change nappies again in his late sixties (she was a career girl, and as he was retired he became the 'househusband'). Well, no sooner did she have that baby but another one popped out, and the upshot is that he had a heart attack last week from which he hasn't recovered, and the funeral is on Friday. The village is buzzing with the rumour that he was taking Niagra, which just goes to show what happens if you try to burn the candle at both ends. Certainly, since it happened, the queue at the chemist's has gone down considerably, and his old golfing cronies are looking far less jaunty.

I know that you were once 'fond' of him, so in the circumstances, if you do want to pay your respects at the service, which is at three in the afternoon, you could stay overnight with me on the put-you-up in the living room. I have already checked the buses and trains and found that there is no way you could get back afterwards, unless you spend the night on the platform at Nottingham, where you'd have to change.

Incidentally, since I'm writing anyway, I thought I'd just mention that I found your swimming costume the other week rolled up inside my old pacamac which I was about to donate to the Village Minellium Bus Shelter fund. I told you there would be a perfectly good explanation for its disappearance, which did not involve me stealing it either to wear myself or to make you less attractive on the beach next to me. I won't enclose it now as it would be a waste of postage stamps if you're coming over next week, and anyway, as you'll see for yourself, the elastic has gone in the legs. When I think of all the trouble it caused! But far be it from me to point the finger of

6

blame, or to rake up ancient history, and anyway, the red wine came out of my cream skirt on the third wash, so as far as *I'm* concerned, the hatchet is well and truly buried.

Can you let me know of your intentions either way as soon as possible so I can give young Tracey Snapes an idea of numbers?

Best wishes,

Irene Spencer

Sheepdipper's Shed
Shooters Hill
Shale, Shap,
Nr Great Shagthorne
Derbs.

Wed.

Dear Irene,

I was covered in shame on receipt of your letter. (I was also covered in sheep's yoghurt— your opening phrase was so alarming, I thought it was one of those dreadful chain letters which plague the vulnerable, and I dropped the hand-thrown pot all over me.) Shame, because it's been on my mind to write to you for months, particularly after I found several photos of us on that very holiday when I was clearing my room at the nursing home. Remember that lovely Italian man who insisted on snapping us at the Trevi fountain? You had just called me a blithering idiot for tossing in the equivalent of five pounds in lire. Foreign coins are so confusing. He caught what I like to think is the essential you, grimacing, with your handbag raised as though you were about to strike me. I did have a laugh, and it put me in mind of so many

8

similar occasions over the years we have known each other.

As you see, I am at Howard's. I came here after a brief sojourn at 'Golden Pastures' residential home. I'd had a nasty bout of flu which led to slight deafness, but Karen decided my blank stare when she was screaming something about her latest love tangle was incipient Alzheimer's and persuaded Howard to commit me to long-term care for the elderly. Lord save us from over-dramatic daughters! I got my hearing back and left after a fortnight, though I must say I was tempted to stay longer—it was very pleasant to have all one's meals prepared, even though the cocoa did taste funny. I am now waiting for sheltered accommodation to become vacant. I suppose that means waiting for one of the poor old dears to die, talking of funerals. I never thought I would wish it on anybody, but life at Sheepdipper's Shed, even with one's favourite child, is a little trying. The sheep's yoghurt has not been doing at all well since all that fuss about BSC affecting dairy products and some days I'm at my wits' end as to how to use up sixty gallons. Perhaps I should take a leaf out of Cleopatra's book and bath in it! Might be preferable to tepid, solar-heated water with the pungent aroma of night soil—the toilet facilities here have not improved, despite Howard and his partner, Antony, having created their own personal

9

cesspit.

Poor Bill. A case of what goes around, comes around. Or what goes up must come down, if he really was taking Niagra. Oh, my goodness, I've just realised Friday is the day after tomorrow, they've taken so long to forward your letter. The matron at Golden Pastures is a little disorganised. I once surprised her with a bottle of sherry poised over a mug, at nine-thirty in the morning.

Of course I'll come. It's only proper. Besides, I'm curious for a glance at this Tracey. I'd love to stay, if only for the hot water. I'll taxi to yours from the station and change. Oh dear, what on earth will I wear? Howard went through my wardrobe when I arrived and chucked out everything in man-made fibres. That reminds me, by all means give that bathing costume to the Bus Shelter fund. Perhaps someone with large thighs will buy it. Howard is planning the 'Biggest Party the Derby Dales Has Known' for New Year's Eve '99. He's asked me to help with the catering. At last a use for the yoghurt! I despair at having to think up more recipes, but anything I can do to help the Millennium . . .

Will jump on Howard's bike and pedal this the four miles to the post. (Really, you can take this eco stuff too far. Howard and Antony *do* live up a 1 in 4 hill.) Look forward to seeing you, if I survive it.

All the best,

Vera

The Limes
Saturday

Dear Howard,

It is with great regret that I write to tell you that your mother has had an accident while staying here with me, but is not seriously ill. I have not yet ascertained the exact details of the full circumstances of her fall, as her dentures broke during the incident and her lips have swollen up like balloons, so she's making even less sense than usual. Suffice it to say that, as usual, the combination of strong drink and a member of the opposite sex had a disastrous effect on her. And not only on her. The 'gentleman' in question fortunately escaped with a black eye and a broken toe, but Tracey Snapes's pelargoniums will never be the same again. And all of this during the baked meats of Tracey's husband's funeral! I was so embarrassed I didn't know where to put myself. But then again, what did I expect? Your Mother has never given me anything but trouble.

The hospital released her because they didn't have a bed, so now neither have I and am forced to make use of my put-you-up in the living room, which with my back is like sleeping on a time bomb. Is there any way you can arrange to take her back to Sheepdipper's Shed to finish her convalescence with you? Quite frankly I'm exhausted, and she's only been here a day and a half. Besides, I'm sure the country air would do her more good than being cooped up here in my bedroom.

Unfortunately there has been a misunderstanding with the cable company and I am currently without a phone, so please write back immediately and let me know what you intend to do. And whatever it is, make it quick.

Hope you're well by the way, and kind regards to Antony.

With all good wishes,

Irene

The Limes
Saturday

Dear Howard,

I don't know what Irene has told you and I
don't want to call her a liar, but it definitely
isn't true. There *was* a small incident, I'll
admit, but nothing like on the scale she has
been suggesting and certainly not for the
reasons!

The funeral was a pleasant enough affair.
Can't say I took much to Tracey Snapes, she's
gone past her bloom very quickly. I'm sure
living with Bill and two small children was no
picnic, or perhaps it was too many! She's put
on so much weight and with her bottle blonde
hair, she reminded me of a chat show hostess.
She'd omitted to follow Bill's last instructions
(no doubt getting even when he can't answer
back) and the wake was an alcohol-free zone.
One of Bill's golfing compadres, Barry
Rowbotham and I were chatting in the
conservatory ... Barry's a smoker, though only
cigars. Needless to say, Tracey didn't have the
heating on and Barry, a charming man, was
kind enough to offer me a drop of warming
whisky in my tea. We soon got tripping down
memory lane about Bill. Barry was a hoot,
showing me some of his tricks with a golf club.

14

(Unfortunately Tracey had left some pelargoniums . . . well, that's what she called them, they looked like common or garden geraniums to me . . . rather too close to the edge of a shelf and three or four did get broken.)

Barry is also a ballroom-dancing champ, he's got international trophies. Unfortunately his partner is in hospital at the moment with several slipped discs and he was telling me how much he missed it. Well, you know how familiar *I* am with the dance floor! In no time he was demonstrating a couple of tricky steps in the Paso Doble, which has always been one of my favourites. Some people might say, indeed they did, and Irene was one of them, that dancing at a funeral shows disrespect. I had to remind her of the many rituals we had seen on our travels where those in mourning were wearing considerably less than a lounge suit and a heliotrope two-piece. However . . .

The tiled floor in the conservatory was unusually slippery, possibly a film of ice due to the freezing temperature, and, executing a flamboyant bull charge, I skidded, stepped on Barry's toe, threw out an arm to save myself and punched him in the eye. Easily done, as I'm sure you'll agree. We both fell to the ground. Irene said afterwards we 'crashed' and 'rolled around on top of one another', but that's a wild exaggeration. I have tried to explain what really happened but my dentures have sustained irreparable damage, which makes speaking difficult and Irene swears she can't read my writing, which after all our years of correspondence is a bit rich. Staying with her, under the circumstances, is very trying and I'd be grateful if you could come and get me as soon as possible. It is awkward to manage the train in plaster.

Irene has just come in and brusquely informed me that it will take six weeks to replace my teeth on the NHS, so I must stop now and attempt to stick them together with some blue-tack. Oh, for a *Blue Peter* for the elderly!

Your loving Mumsie xx

PS Careful with that Niagra . . . Barry tells me it's easy to overdo it. Irene implied that's what we were testing on the conservatory floor.

Sheepdipper's Shed

Monday

Dear Irene

How lovely to hear from you after all this time, albeit in such painful circumstances. Mumsie's letter arrived by the second post, adding to the confusion. I think it's better to correspond directly with you, though, given the Alzheimer's situation. Poor Mumsie, she does have a way of courting disaster. Which limbs did she break exactly? Life on a mountain is tough enough, without milking sheep with both arms in plaster. Even worse if it's her legs. How will she manage a bicycle?

Still, needs must and we won't abandon her. We approached the hospital in Great Shagthorne about an ambulance, but the triage nurse (although he's a pet) said with all her problems she just didn't qualify as salvageable. His advice was a quick pillow over the face, but I'm sure he was only joking!

Antony is talking to our cheese man about borrowing his delivery van. We can lie her full length in that, which is more than we can in the MG Midget! All being well, we'll be with you the day after tomorrow.

17

Fondest regards, and a big kiss for Mumsie
(not on her swollen lips).

Howard

PS We long for something as adult as cable.
Sadly, it hasn't reached the dull old Derby
Dales.

Dear Howard,

Wednesday has come and gone with neither sight nor sound of you. Did you mean you'd be arriving the day after tomorrow from you writing your note, or the day after tomorrow of me receiving it? Quite frankly I am being run ragged here with demands for this and demands for that, and what with your mother's teeth going west and everything having to be puréed, and my blender giving up the ghost and having to do it all by hand through a sieve, and then her having an accident on the bedsheets with the beetroot borscht, I really don't think I could be held responsible if something DREADFUL HAPPENED . . . My blood pressure has ROCKETED and the way I am feeling at the moment one or other of us may be in great danger of death.

I had to pause there. Water was coming through the living-room ceiling on to my head, as you'll notice from the runny ink. She'd fallen asleep in the bath with the tap running and her foot jammed in the overflow. Naturally she survived.

If you haven't arrived tomorrow to take her

away I am afraid I will have to send her on to you in a minicab, COD.

Yours

Irene

Dear Vera,

I hope your journey back to Sheepdipper's went all right in the van last month, and that you survived the smell of the Gorgonzola. And I hope that your leg is feeling better, and that the Bostick on your dentures dried eventually without sticking your gums together as feared. As you will see from the contents of this parcel, you left a couple of undergarments behind, laundered and enclosed. I'm also enc-ing some home made fudge that you should be able to manage to suck even if you still can't chew. I bought it from Mrs Appleyard, who is renowned for her confectionery, at the Home Fayre stall of the Minellium Bus Shelter Bring and Buy yesterday. A couple of people from the funeral were there—Ida Loseby and Mona Postlethwaite, I don't know if you remember them but they remember you—and they asked after you and told me to send you their best.

It's hard to find the words, but I'm hoping that in time the dust may settle on this recent visit of yours, and that we can put behind us our hasty words. I bumped into Barry Rowbotham last week in the supermarket, and he was quick to take all the blame for the incident at the funeral. Thinking about it since—and you know what I'm like for dwelling on things until I've got them thoroughly sorted through—I've realised it was inevitable that we would get tense with each other at Bill's funeral, after all the trouble he caused between us so long ago. It was two years before we managed to speak again after I found you in bed together, if you remember, and—you may not know this, for you certainly didn't hear it from me—he had asked me only the day before if I'd consider taking the marital plunge. I really think that, all things being equal, if we could get over that, we can get over this.

In pensive mood I got out all your old letters today, and some rough copies of mine (I always like to neaten up mistakes afterwards, and usually make a fair copy of my missives) and I realised that the only time we have trouble between us is when we are actually together in the flesh. I was reminded how much I miss your cheery letters when we're at loggerheads and not speaking. I don't know what it is about you, but I just seem to find you more palatable in print.

Can bygones be bygone? Could we stick to the written word, do you think, and resist the temptation to meet? As you pointed out once in one of your notelets, there is a relief in being able to confide in someone outside the daily circle. I know for my part that it's nice to

22

think that, after unburdening oneself, one's most sensitive secrets will not be touring the village before one can even get back home after being probed in the post office by wagging tongues and flapping ears. (Rereading that, I find it to be what I think they call a mixed metaphor, but I am putting it in my fair copy because I can't think how it would be better, and I think you'll understand.)

Vera, it's hard to say it, but I'm sorry for my part if I caused offence during your stay. I was tetchy and under some strain. There. Now to the post box with this before I change my mind. Time will tell if you feel the same.

With fond regards and hopeful thoughts,

Your erstwhile friend

Irene

The Homely Faggot
Western Esplanade
Vicker-upon-St Agnes

Friday

Dear Irene,

Really, I've never known anyone like you
for meeting trouble half-way. Except perhaps
Audrey Roscoe. As you can see I am staying
with her to recuperate. I'd had all I could take
of Sheepdipper's. Howard would insist on
plunging my leg in sheep's urine. Some ethnic
health practice Antony picked up. Thank
goodness they didn't extend it to the dentures.

Anyway, you will be pleased to know I am
much better. In fact, as Karen said when I saw
her last week and expressed surprise at her
tattoo—apparently she's had it two years—
'Mother's back to normal.'

Speaking of memory loss, of course I
remember Ida and Mona. Ida's the one whose
husband was a transvestite and Mona's the one
you said looked like a teletubby. But I don't
recall what these 'words' were. You insisted
you couldn't understand a thing I said, hasty or
otherwise. Certainly *you* raised your voice
more than was strictly necessary. But I put that
down to your distress over Bill. I am more

sensitive than you realise. I know perfectly well you've been carrying a candle for that two-timing creep for years and, in my opinion, it's a good thing he's dead. Especially living so close to you. Now you can move on with your life, Irene, instead of hoping he will ever come back. You've missed a lot of chances. There was that nice Italian policeman on our trip, and the mechanic who mended the Dormobile . . .

Audrey's just come back in with the fish and news that there's sheltered accommodation going near the beach. I shall pop down tomorrow and investigate. All for now and rest assured your secrets are safe with me. And Audrey Roscoe.

Love, as always,

Vee

Saturday

Dear Irene,

Just had to send you a card with the good news. I got the accommodation! It's not exactly sheltered, unless you count the cliff, but it is near the beach. In fact it's on it. The last incumbent, poor soul, went out for a paddle and never came back. It's an ill wind . . . I am now the proud tenant of a caravan. It's in a large park with all mod cons and facilities . . . bet you can't wait to visit!

Vee

PS Write care of Audrey Roscoe

Lodge 202
Far Shores Trailer Park
Vicker-upon-St Agnes

Sunday

Dear Howard,

Thanks for forwarding Irene's letter. What happened to the undies and home-made fudge? I can't think either would be much use at Sheepdipper's, what with your aversion to nylon and Antony's to sugar. Perhaps you could send them now, so I can put Irene's mind at rest. What an old misery guts she is!

Actually I shall need a few more of my possessions, as you'll be glad to hear I have found a place to live. At least temporarily. There is a transient feel to a 'mobile home', though it's up to its axles in concrete. I want cleaning equipment, wellington boots and the ghetto-blaster. Perhaps you could store the rest in the barn, as the space here is quite limited.

Your ever-loving Mumsie xx

Tuesday

Dear Vera,

Is there *anyone* in your acquaintance who is as perfect as you? In the first few lines of your letter you manage to insult me, your only begotten son, Howard, and his 'partner', and poor old Audrey Roscoe. Strange, since the one thing that we have in common is that we have all recently extended the hand of friendship to you and put you up—leave aside putting up with you.

I don't know *where* to start with your wild and inaccurate observations. I have not been 'carrying a candle' for Bill (or a torch, for that matter, which I believe is the usual nomenclature). As far as I'm concerned, it was over before it had begun, practically. It is true that I was once foolish enough to feel warmly towards him all those years ago when he first became my 'gentleman friend', but once you and he started to see each other behind my back, it was over and out as far as I was concerned. Do I need to remind you of the country hotel weekend break for three, where I discovered the two of you wrapped around each other and canoodling in the king-size four-poster? As Marjorie Proops once wrote to a woman unfortunate enough to have been

28

in my position, one expects such faithlessness from men, but from a woman friend, never! The reason I was tense at his funeral was because it reminded me of *your* betrayal, not his.

As for me now being able to move on in life and missing lots of chances, may I remind you that the only reason that that 'nice Italian policeman' (incidentally, they are called *carabinieri* in their language—so named because of their rifles—you'd know that if you'd paid more attention to the culture of the countries we passed through, instead of singing 'Viva Espagna' and 'The Chicken Song' at every bar and disco you could find that served baked beans on toast)—where was I? Oh, yes . . . The only reason he became interested in me was because I had to flutter my lashes at him to stop you being shot. You had had far too much to drink and you were driving at twice the speed limit down the *autostrada* with a paper bag over your head, because, you said (or screamed, as I remember), you 'couldn't stand the sight of me any more'. Likewise the mechanic had to be mollified because we hadn't enough money to pay him for the repairs. If you call that, or similar, 'moving on in life' I don't wonder you are now living in a caravan park. And speaking of which, I don't know why you want me to correspond with you care of Audrey. If you think for one minute that I would visit you if you gave me your address, then you obviously didn't understand a single word of my letter.

Last, and by no means least, I don't know where you get the idea that Ida's husband is a transvestite. He wears bells on his trousers and a funny hat because he is a Morris dancer and that is all. Perhaps you have been hanging around Sheepdipper's for too long.

I notice you don't thank me for laundering your smalls, or for the fudge, but perhaps you are sent such gifts every day of the week and therefore don't think it worthy of comment.

I was very sorry to read of the fate of the previous incumbent of your caravan. As you say, that poor woman's tragedy is your gain—but then that seems to be how life goes for you, doesn't it? I shall think of you when you are moving into your new home, and hope that all goes well.

Happy paddling.

Kind regards,

Irene

Tuesday

Dear Audrey,

I hope you don't mind being a 'poste restaurante', but Vera asked me to write to her c/o you. Would you mind very much giving her the enc. missive?

I hope you have been having jolly times together. She is great fun, of course, and so brave, considering what she has to put up with. I don't know whether she has told you, since she is the last one to ask for sympathy, but her only son is 'gay' and her daughter is a single mother, so it's hardly surprising she sometimes needs the solace of another woman's husband or lover. It's so sad to think that her memory is going. She told me in her last letter that she hadn't known her daughter was tattooed, but Karen has had 'Mum' on one hand and 'Hate' on the other for ages since.

I know I can rely on your discretion not to spread any of this around, now that she is trying to 'move on in life' and make her new home in your town.

Hope you are keeping well.

Kindest regards,

Irene Spencer

31

Thursday

Irene,

It has come to my ears that you have been spreading malicious gossip about me. Audrey Roscoe popped down to the park this afternoon to tell me herself. Apparently my children are 'odd' as the result of an abusive childhood, my grandchild is illegitimate and my husband died in mysterious circumstances after learning I was a serial adulterer.

Speaking of which, you are someone to complain of 'wild and inaccurate observations'! My so-called 'affair' with Bill Snapes is a total ligament of your imagination. As I think I told you at the time, our being in bed together was a mistake from start to finish. There I was, as I thought, on a weekend break you had booked for you, me and Bill as three 'swinging singles', and I find myself in the Honeymoon Suite with a man I've barely been introduced to. (Though come to think of it, I could say the same for the first night I spent with my husband Gerald.) It was all your fault for booking the blithering Honeymoon Suite to begin with! It had more doors than a French farce. What with the separate bathrooms, walk-in wardrobes and dimness of lighting, it's a wonder Bill and I found our way to the bed at all. As it was a 'King-size', we were peacefully slumbering at either side, without even knowing the other was there. I don't know which of the three of us was the more surprised when we woke up and found you wedged between us. I can recall to this day your fury. You were white-faced even through your make-up.

You tried to pass it off as a mistake the hotel had made, but who goes to bed in false eyelashes and bright pink lipstick, except in an advert? It was quite clear you had intended all along to end up in the bridal suite with Bill, and only the lateness of your train meant I got there before you.

Fortunately this is all *de rigueur* in a trailer park. If anything, it has raised my profile. I saw several people in the communal facilities pointing and staring with awe on their faces. (On reflection, that could have been owing to the state of my undies. The ones you returned are a violent shade of puce. Did you wash them with the beetroot borscht sheets? The fudge, by the way, finally put paid to my dentures. On contact with it, the Bostick melted.)

But—as I was saying—although it makes little difference here, apart from a visit from Victim Support and an invitation to bare all in the local paper, I don't want this outrageous slander all over St Agnes! I dread to think what could have happened if that letter had got into the wrong hands. I'm at a loss to understand your motives. All I have ever tried to be is a friend to you.

As such, I have discussed your perfidy with Site Security. Audrey got it wrong—this accommodation is not sheltered, it is 'protected' and he says for a small sum *he* will pay *you* a visit.

Yours,

Vera

PS His name is Damon, but not for nothing is he known as 'Demon'. The last person who caused bother to a resident is still in traction.

Lodge 202
Far Shores Trailer Park
Vicker-upon-St Agnes

Thursday

Dear Howard,

Sorry to be a bother, but could you return that £250 I lent you to install the Jacuzzi? I wouldn't ask you unless it was a matter of urgent family honour.

Mother

The Limes

Saturday

Dear Vera,

I don't know what to make of the wild and ridiculous assertations in your last, but I believe I have mentioned before about what an old stirrer Audrey Roscoe is. I have certainly never ever told anybody that the circumstances of Gerald's death were 'mysterious'. How could I, when I didn't even know myself until you just told me in your letter?

I will certainly not stoop to address your 'false memory syndrome' about our so-called 'three-in-a-bed' situation with Bill Snapes. Suffice it to say *I* thought it was buried in the past, but obviously you still enjoy getting it out for further inspection and rejigging of facts.

As for threatening me with a gorilla attack from a hired assassin, I can only think that you have embraced the lurid ethos of the trailer park you talk so proudly of with eager arms. Do not for one moment think that I am frightened by these scare tactics—I am merely hurt to have my friendship so rebuffed.

Goodbye, and good luck with the rest of

your life,

Irene Spencer

The Limes

Saturday

Dear Lesley,

I have been thinking about you so much lately, and realise that it is selfish of me to let a little thing like fear of flying put me off visiting you in Melbourne. I don't wonder you have begged me to come out there on a visit so many times—it must be difficult now Keith has left you and you are having to juggle the demands of motherhood with working for your living. And if I don't come soon, little Cheryl Marie won't know her dear old Granny Spencer!

I have been looking into the rigmarole of getting a flight and insurance and applying for a visa and sorting things out this end so I can come for a good long stay, and find that unfortunately I won't be able to be with you before this coming Wednesday.

All my love, dear,

Mummy xxx

Dear Irene,

Can you ever forgive me? I don't know what came over me. Trailer-park dementia is the only excuse I can offer. I'm afraid they all watch far too many hysterical TV soaps and then tailor their lives accordingly. The stories I could tell you, and I've only been here a fortnight! My next-door neighbour, Yasmin, has had her patio dug up three times by police looking for parts of her common law husband. She says she wouldn't mind them finding him, he still owes her £48.50, but I presume she means in one piece, alive and kicking—which by all accounts he did frequently. Speaking of kicking, from the couple on the other side I hear constant screaming and shouting. One night I could stand it no more and went round to beg them to stop. I found him handcuffed to the bunk bed and her, dressed head to toe in black PVC, slapping him about with a fish slice. This was an unexpected view of marital abuse, but when I threatened to call social services they laughed. Apparently they were making material for 'surfers' to 'download' from the 'net'. They explained I was now on

39

video and if I wanted to stay and join in they'd split the proceeds with me. There must be quite a taste for this sort of thing, they've got a socking great Mercedes parked outside. Which reminds me, I must tell Howard . . .

But I digress. I am really writing to apologise for my threatening letter and, even worse, for following it up in reality. Imagine my surprise and distress when Damon returned with the news that the house was locked and shuttered and the neighbours had told him you had fled the country! As he said himself, there was no need for that. He has 'nuff respec' for someone of your great age and the most he would have done was 'trash' your flower beds. He's actually rather sweet and most days pops round to check I'm all right and collect his five pounds. Yesterday he offered to pierce my navel. I'm sure it was kindly meant and not because I didn't have any change on me.

I have just realised I have no idea where to send this. Where are you, Irene? Perhaps you're scared to tell me, but you need have no fear of further reprisals. I couldn't possibly afford to give Damon another £250. Well, I will address it to your former home in the hopes somebody knows your whereabouts. Oh—I can see the postman hovering the other side of the barbed wire. He won't deliver on the site because of Damon's pit bull terrier.

Later:
The post brought a card from Karen telling me you have gone to Australia! This was followed by a tirade of abuse which, I presume, blames me. But I've suffered so many over the years that as soon as I got to 'selfish, thoughtless, vile, ignorant, etc., etc.' I ceased reading. No address, so I shall stick to plan A. Damon will chase down the postman. He has a Countryman Range Rover with four-wheel drive and bullbars, which I think is a charming image in a trailer park.

I do hope this finds you, my dear, and that all is not lost. I understand you can wander for days in the Outback, with only 'swaggermen' and dingoes for company.

Once more, many apologies and all my love,

Vera

19 Byron Street,
St Urban
Melbourne
VICTORIA

Monday

Dear Vera,

Your letter has finally caught up with me and I have paid the excess postage it cost to send it on here. Fortunately, since it only contained one sheet of paper and 'all your love' it didn't weigh very much.

I have thought long and hard as to whether to reply, but then I remembered it was coming up to your birthday (at least if you're posting from Australia), so I have decided to risk it and send you a card. If you've been threatening all your friends with bodily harm lately, it may be the only one you get. I note you still don't enclose your full address, so I shall have to send it to the trailer park and hope it finds you. I can hardly credit the life you describe there, and only hope you are happy at last to have found your level.

I am having a wonderful time here with my daughter, Lesley, and am so glad to be able to spend so much 'quality time' with my little granddaughter, Cheryl Marie. I really don't

42

know how Lesley managed without me. It must be heart-breaking for you missing your own granddaughter's childhood, what with you being constantly at loggerheads with Karen. She wrote me a lovely long letter the other week, incidentally, full of fun as usual. She's thinking of coming out here on a visit.

I hope you won't be too lonely spending your birthday on your own, but at least on your caravan site it won't be dull, by the sounds of it. Karen told me that she definitely wouldn't be spending it with you this year (she phrased it rather differently, actually, but that was the gist), and she didn't think Howard and Antony would be either. Actually Lesley and I will be going to a beach barbecue with some friends on the day itself, so I will raise a glass of chilled 'Yarrunga Field' to wish you well.

All for now, as I must trot off and pick up Cheryl Marie from kindergarten and get something for our tea. Poor Lesley is worked off her feet at the estate agency, and has to spend an incredible amount of evenings dining with clients—she often gets home after midnight quite exhausted, poor lamb.

Happy birthday.

Regards,

Irene

43

Sunday

Dearest Irene,

How wonderful to hear from you after all this time. I thought you were dead. Perhaps savaged by kangaroos. I saw a programme on Discovery about them and apparently they can turn quite nasty. Trust Karen not to tell me she has been corresponding with you all this time! She was always very secretive when she was a child. I only found out she knew about babies (though, in the light of events, clearly not enough) by reading her diary.

Thank you for the birthday greetings— sweet of you to remember. Personally, I'd rather not at my age. But this year I didn't have a choice. Yasmin and Carol—did I mention her? She's the one who's involved in 'net' mail order videos—decided to give me a party. Yasmin does tarot readings, so of course she knew the date and she'd arranged a wonderful surprise with all the park residents. She'd even invited Howard and Karen— needless to say, their names had come up in my reading—Howard as the Hanging Man and

Karen as the Death card.

The whole of the park was decorated with bunting—I later found out Yasmin's children had 'borrowed' it from the promenade—and there was a fabulous barbecue on *our* beach. It was a chilly night but it warmed up when we roasted half a cow and twenty pounds of sausages. Carol's got an arrangement with the local butcher, something to do with the videos. Of course 'hooch' from Dave and Barbra's 'still' helped. They make a fiery concoction in an old tin bath in the lean-to which used to house their Elsan. The only thing that was 'chilled' (in Damon's parlance) at my barbecue was the guest list. In fact the party was 'kicking', to use the word for once in a less unpleasant connotation. Karen never appeared, which was a pity as Yasmin had offered a forecast. I forecast she wouldn't come, which hardly makes me psychic. But, despite a breakdown—possibly the car or possibly Antony, who was in tears—Howard and Antony arrived in time for the fireworks, a stunning display of Damon's home-made pyrotechnics. Speaking of 'bangers', the site is littered with them. Several flew through the air, along with Howard's toupee and the remains of the cow. Howard is now thinking of employing Damon for his Millennium bash, as he can always lay his hands on Semtex.

I'm so looking forward to the millennium. Yasmin has prophesied a high time here. I

45

prophesy it will be in more ways than one if Damon has anything to do with it! Have you made any plans yet? What exactly is the religion in Australia?

Anyway, my dear, I'm baby-sitting Yasmin's children while she takes part in a 'Mystic Fayre'. I won't get a word written there—I need both hands free for them—so I'll finish.

Oh, Irene, I *have* missed your letters. I've told everyone here so much about you, Yasmin could do you an absent reading! Do keep in touch now, I'm longing to hear more about your life in Oz.

Love,

Vera

Down Under

Tuesday night, or is it Wednesday morning?

Dear Vera,

Thank you for your vivid account of your birthday celebrations—it sounded very pleasant if that is your preference for conviviality. It has been my birthday today—don't feel guilty about not sending a card whatever you do, it really couldn't matter less—and I have had the most wonderful time sampling the fruits of the New World vineyards. To make up for me having to baby-sit tonight while she, poor love, had to go to dinner with yet another client, Lesley bought me a case of Victorian wines all to myself. That's wines made in the state of Victoria, by the by, not during the late Queen's reign—took me a while to work that one out. I may be a little tipsy, so please excuse the writing.

Now to satisfy your curiosity about Australia. It is very big for starters, and very far away from everywhere else. The flight over is horrendous—a whole day in the air, can you imagine?—with a couple of hours off for good behaviour in Bangkok airport. You have your dinner and then watch two films and then go

47

to sleep (those who can relax enough to do so) and then have breakfast, and then you look out of the window (those who are brave enough to do so) and see Australia, and then you keep flying across it for hours and hours and hours before you get to Melbourne, which is where Lesley moved to after she split up with Keith, and where there are no kangaroos, incidentally, and no dingoes either, fortunately for little Cheryl Marie.

Here, you have to think of everything upside down. A north-facing garden means as much to them as a south-facing one does to us, being in the other hemisphere. Melbourne is down south and Melburnians are very proud of their weather. They will tell you, at the drop of a hat, that they can have all four seasons in any given day. Depending on which way the wind blows, it can bring the chill of the Antarctic or the heat of the countryside (or 'bush' as they call it here). Today, for example, I set off for a stroll along the beach in glorious sunshine, only to be hit by hailstones the size of tennis balls on the way back. Believe me, a parasol is no defence against Antarctic ice.

But speaking of tennis balls, I must tell you about the Sausage Sizzle I went to at the weekend, held by the local tennis club to attract 'veterans' to start going to play in the afternoons. Of course I hadn't been in whites for many a long year, but fortunately there was a group of novices like myself so I joined their number. There was one lady there who reminded me of you, actually—very jolly, but my, she suffered in the heat with all her bulk. Anyway, there was a lovely man there called Vincent—retired, a widower, very nicely turned out and with a full head of hair and beautifully shaped hands. I think even his teeth are his own. As things fell out, we partnered each other most of the afternoon and got on very well, and though Lesley's house is really not far from the club, he insisted on giving me a lift home. When it emerged in casual conversation that it was going to be my birthday in a couple of days, he suggested he take me out to lunch. (Actually, he suggested dinner, but what with Lesley's busy schedule I knew I couldn't count on having the night off.) Which is where I've been today. He'd booked us into a very exclusive restaurant at the harbour with a wonderful view and no expense spared. I had oysters, crayfish and three kinds of chocolate mousse, and it was superb. It was so lovely to have the company of a man again, and he's so much better looking than Bill. Unfortunately he has to visit his grandchildren for a few days now, but we've arranged to play tennis again next Wednesday.

Just got up to let Lesley in, and fell down. All now. Bit tiddly. Tell more about Australia next time. Felt all right before, but standing was mistake. Remind me to tell you about the possum.

Love from your pal,

Inebriated Irene (joke—ha ha!) xxxxxx

Lodge 202 etc.

Friday

My dear Irene,

How remiss of me to forget your birthday! Really, sometimes I wonder if Karen isn't right about the state of my brain, though it goes against the grain to admit it. Enclosed is a Birthday Tarot from Yasmin, which I gave her all the data to prepare. Funnily enough I remembered that perfectly! I had to guess the time of birth of course, but I do recall you telling me your mother cursed you for arriving when she was at her lowest ebb, so I imagine that was about four in the morning.

Yasmin also brought this little news article which, having done your reading, she thought might be of interest. Perhaps you had better show it to 'Vincent'! (Keep on with the booze, then you won't go all buttoned up on him—men like a chatty woman.) Oz really does sound like the land of change. Especially the weather.

Talking of hailstones, I am off to Sheepdipper's for the weekend. It's Howard and Antony's anniversary and they are having a 'Do'. Howard wants a hand with the catering—plenty of sizzling sausages—it's a

51

Fork and Finger event.

There's life in us old girls yet, eh? Promise to write fully on my return.

Love,

Vee

PS Don't forget the possum!

Vicker-upon-St Agnes *Star*

The secret to a long and healthy life is SEX! Sex keeps people young and vibrant and halts the ageing process, according to Dr Raj Garibaldi, who insists, 'Ageless national icons like Margaret Thatcher and the Queen Mother are leading very vigorous sex lives.'

St Urban

Tuesday

Dear Vera,

Sorry it's been a few weeks since writing. I'm afraid in the interim I've mislaid your last letter, so I can't remember if there were any questions therein. I do seem to remember you appeared to be obsessed with sex, which is a shame in an older person, I always think, and more often seems to afflict the men, as in 'dirty old' etc. Have you started back on the UHT again, I wonder? I really don't think it suits you.

Thank you for the Birthday Tarot reading from your new friend Yasmin (is that a Romany name?), which I found today at the back of my underwear drawer. I didn't know they needed birth dates and times for the cards—I thought that was Astrology? Anyway, if they do and if it is important to the accuracy, that explains why it makes no sense to me at all—you've got my birth year down so wrong that I'd be eighty-three! Was that your little joke or her bad handwriting? Certainly I have never seen myself as having a 'burning, passionate nature, hidden beneath a cool exterior which aches to be torn down'. I would consider myself to be almost the opposite, in fact—at least as far as any tearing down goes. At any rate, I can see what Karen means about your memory.

Did I mention in my last that I have joined a tennis club? I now play two afternoons a week, partnered by a charming gentleman called Vincent. He is a widower, very fit and active for his years, with a full head of hair and all his own teeth. He used to be in hosiery, I believe. Imagine my surprise when he insisted on taking me out to lunch on my birthday! We went to a very exclusive harbourside restaurant and ate oysters and crayfish and three kinds of wine (including a champagne), one to go with each course. The wine here is very good— much better than European. Lesley bought me a mixed case for my birthday as an introduction to New World vinny culture, but there seem to be so many to learn! On the couple of occasions that I've managed to get a Sunday off (Lesley works most weekends and so I usually look after Cheryl Marie), Vincent has driven me out to local vineyards for tastings and lunch, and I have availed myself of his having a four-wheel drive to buy several cases to sample at my leisure.

It's no use. I've got to stop. The ruddy possum is at it again and I just can't concentrate for the racket. Remind me to tell you about it another time.

Write soon,

Irene

Lodge 202
Far Shores Trailer Park
Vicker-upon-St Agnes

Thursday . . . or Friday

Dear Irene,

I started a letter to you ages ago but I've quite forgotten where I put it. Incidentally, you did mention Vincent, the tennis club, the teeth, the lunch, the oysters, the crayfish and the wine in your last one. Perhaps you should go easy on the New World 'vinny culture'—is that an Australian expression?

Wrong date or not, I thought Yasmin's description of you was completely accurate, though she did mention part of your trouble was accepting it. Where on earth do you get the idea that I am sex-obsessed? I haven't given it a thought in days, and no, I'm not on UHT, but I'm sure this genetically modified food has a lot to answer for. Howard won't touch it. He insists it has the opposite effect to increasing sex drive and in fact may be leading to the men growing breasts and wanting to have babies.

Which reminds me, I was writing to you about his 'Do', which gave a whole new meaning to 'fork and finger'. I didn't know it was possible to attach so much metal to body parts. One of his guests appeared to be wearing an entire canteen of cutlery. Outside of a boot fair, I've never seen so much fingering in public—and as for the 'sizzling sausages'! Clearly no one there was eating GM foods, though of course, being Howard's, there was plenty of soya. I'm still shockable, it seems, despite everything we see nowadays on television.

The most important news is that Karen was there with her little girl, Sabrina. It was the first time I'd seen them in over a year, and my, how Sabrina has grown. She is a charming little thing and soon got used to calling me Granny. When I arrived she didn't seem to know who I was, and asked if it was me who Mummy called 'the mad old bat'. When Karen heard I was living in a trailer park, she laughed raucously and said I'd graduated from soap opera to cartoon, whatever that means. Anyway, being homeless again she decided to come and stay, though of course I pointed out that space was limited.

The first morning was very awkward. I'd put up a curtain to give her some privacy, but she still sleeps till lunchtime and I needed to get to the kitchenette, so I popped my head round and asked if she wanted some 'brunch'. She swore loudly and said, 'Give me a chance to put my knickers on before you start stuffing food down me.' I admit I was hurt. I said, 'I don't seem to be able to do a thing right these days,' to which she responded, 'Crashing in on a person when they're half-naked is never "right", Mother, and you've been doing it for sixty-five years.' She is as rude as ever and, besides, how does she know? I've only been doing it to her for thirty-five of them. This morning she staggered up and snapped off my favourite classical music radio programme, saying it 'did her head in'. She's been here a month and if she doesn't go soon, it will do *my* head in.

How do you manage with Lesley? Perhaps it's easier because she's out all the time. Whatever kind of a job requires seven days a week? I hope she is getting good bonuses. I'd be glad if Karen got any job at all. My pension won't stretch to the luxuries she demands. She's just given me a list which includes Java coffee beans, gravadlax, luxury shower gel and a mobile phone. I shall have to speak to Damon.

All for now—it's time to pick Sabrina up from school. She is lodging next door with Carol and Terry.

Write soon, I need support!

Lots of love,

Vera

PS What on earth's going on with the possum?

Dear Vera,

Thank you for your newsy letter. I won't
bother to tell you any more about my lovely
outings with Vincent if it causes offence, and I
do so apologise, I'm sure, if I've been boring
you with my repetition. (By the by, speaking of
which, although you claim not to be obsessed
with 'sex', I notice you managed to cram it in
twice in one paragraph.) I can't imagine where
you get the idea that my repeating myself has
anything to do with drink, as I am just a social
drinker, as you well know. It's simply old age
and can't be helped. As I keep having to
explain to Lesley, 'Wait till it happens to you!'
I only wish I could be there to say, 'I told you
so,' when her little brain isn't as sharp as it is
now.

How funny that we're both involved in
looking after our grandchildren at the
moment. Having children is much nicer the
second time round, don't you find? Or maybe
it's just that Cheryl Marie is an easier child
than Lesley was. Incidentally, you ask what
type of job she has, although I'm sure I've
mentioned several times (perhaps *you're* the
one who's drinking too much and killing off

brain cells!). She is an estate agent, and things are done very differently here in Australia as far as house sales go. Instead of making individual appointments for buyers to see properties, they have an open time at weekends. The owner has to leave for an hour or so, while one of the agents shows people round and gives the patter, so here they really work for their commission. Also, nearly all properties are auctioned, not just the ones that are falling down and hard to get rid of like in England, so Saturdays and Sundays Lesley's either showing houses or out selling them under her hammer. The auctions are held outside the property in the street and are quite exciting. Usually they have a dummy bidder just to start the ball rolling, and my services have been called upon in this respect a couple of times. I felt almost as nervous as if I was really buying!

You ask me to tell you about the possum, but I'm sure I already have. When you see them in the garden they're really very sweet, so you wouldn't mind them living in the attic if it wasn't for them doing their 'business' through the ceiling . . .

You wouldn't believe it, just as I was writing about it! You'd almost think they could read your thoughts. Right on my head this time, and all over this letter! Well, I'm sorry, I haven't got time to write it out again—this is already my fair copy. I've dabbed it with kitchen paper and that will have to do. It's just lucky I'm using Biro instead of pen and ink. And now I shall have to shampoo my hair before picking up little Cheryl Marie from school, and ring Pete the Possum up again to make another appointment, and scrub the sofa and rug. And here I am supposed to be enjoying my retirement and being cosseted a bit myself in my old age! A woman's work is never done, Vera, particularly if she is a grandmother!

Do give Karen my love, and tell her I'll be replying to her letter soon. What a pity you haven't been getting on better. She's such a lovely girl. Isn't it great that she and Damon seem to be hitting it off?

All for now. Take care.

Love,

Irene xx

Lodge 202
Far Shores Trailer Park
Vicker-upon-St Agnes

Monday

Dear Irene,

I didn't know a thing about Karen and
Damon 'hitting it off' until Karen announced
they were going to St Tropez for the weekend.
Apparently Damon has associates in
protection on a caravan site there. I was, to
coin one of her phrases, 'gobsmacked'.
Needless to say, I was expected to look after
Sabrina. Not that it was any hardship—she
really is delightful. I can always get a cuddle
from her. Karen was such an unrewarding
child in that department. She would go as stiff
as a board whenever I attempted to touch her.
I can only assume Damon does not encounter
the same problem.

I've taken advantage of her absence to move
Sabrina in with me. To be honest, I'd become
a little concerned at her boarding with Carol
and Terry, what with them being in the sex
video business. Sabrina kept appearing with
new shoes and chocolate, and one hears such
terrible things nowadays. Besides, I just
couldn't stand having Karen as a guest a

moment longer. She has turned my little dwelling upside down, just when I'd got it how it suits me. When she returns (if she ever does—they went for three days and have already been gone a fortnight) she will have to make her own arrangements. Perhaps, given her history, *she* should move in with Carol and Terry.

I have now reorganised the space so Sabrina has her own little bedroom and play area, and without Karen's fourteen boxes of cosmetics— including a do-it-yourself piercing kit—I can now get into my own bathroom! I'm considering getting an extension built on. Dave next door but one has offered to do it. My days revolve around Sabrina's needs, and I admit it's given me a new lease of life. Howard always said I was lost if I couldn't be a carer. I think that nice Jack Straw is right about appointing surrogate grannies. Perhaps his own childhood was deprived of one.

By the way, I know what you mean about 'business'. What with the dogs, cats, goats and chickens, the site is littered with it. The other day Sabrina came in and said she'd been playing 'marbles'. Imagine my disgust when I found they were dried rabbit pellets!

Friday

Karen returned, very brown, last night, and informed me she was moving in with Damon.

64

On reflection I am not surprised. They are two of a kind. Especially in their tastes. They came back with the Range Rover stacked with booze and his and her Rolex watches. She wants Sabrina to move in with them. Over my dead body.

Must stop—it's Sabrina's bath time, then I read her a story. When she arrived, all her books were about one-parent families and children brought up by 'same-sex couples'. We're so enjoying *The Wind in the Willows*.

Huggies, as Sabrina says,

Vee

PS I enclose a photo of Sabrina and me taken by Carol. Do send some of you and Cheryl Marie. And the possum!

Sunday

Dear Vera,

Thank you for your last. I notice you started it on the Monday and finished it on the Friday. Is that because it was an awful chore, or did you mislay it? I hope it was the latter, although I wouldn't wish memory loss on anybody, not even my worst enemy. You'd think I was gaga the way Lesley goes on when I can't think of a word.

And speaking of gaga, how on earth can you compare possum piddle to rabbit pellets? Do you think we have a hole in the ceiling for it to pooh through? Its Number Ones came dripping down on my head when I was writing last time, not its Number Twos. I can't believe I'm having to write this and be so explicit. Trust you. We've had Pete the Possum round twice now, but it just seems to find its way in again. They put a trap in the attic with a bit of apple as bait. You know when it's been caught, because it bangs the cage about like billy-o. The first time it happened I thought we'd got burglars and I phoned the police—I did feel a fool!

66

Thank you for the photograph of Sabrina. What a sweet little girl she's proving to be, and so like her Granny Small—she certainly got your nose! Here's one of Cheryl Marie taken at a fancy dress. She's the one dressed as Little Bo Peep. She's such a little actress and yet so practical! See how she's taken the telescope from Captain Cook to look for her sheep. (Captain Cook was the Englishman who discovered Australia, but if you ask me it couldn't have been very difficult. After all, the Aborigines had already been living there for thousands of years, so they must have found it easily enough.)

I've just returned from another wonderful day out with Vincent. He's such a lovely man and such good company. He won't let me do a thing for myself when we're together—he even opens the car door for me and makes sure I'm settled nicely before he goes all the way round to get in himself. The only time Clive did that was once when we were courting, and then he slammed the door on my leg. Vincent keeps talking about us going away for a weekend, but I don't know how Lesley would manage without me if we did. She's out at work so much, poor dear, that we hardly ever see each other—we communicate by notes. It's not so much like having a daughter, it's more like having another pen-pal!

I had a super postcard from Karen from St Tropez telling me all about her exciting news. I bet you can't wait, and Sabrina must be over the moon! I often worry about Cheryl Marie, being an only. Lesley was, of course, and I'm afraid she got very spoilt as a result. Don't be worried about Damon being wayward—as I said to Karen in my last, this might be just the thing to settle him down.

All for now. Hope this finds you as it leaves me—pleasantly exhausted after a thoroughly enjoyable day.

Fondest thoughts,

Irene

Lodge 202
Far Shores Trailer Park

Friday

Dear Vera . . . I mean Irene,

I'm so upset I've forgotten my own name now! Thank you for informing me in your last of Karen's 'exciting news'. It was certainly more than *she* had bothered to do. Odd to be told of your daughter's pregnancy via Australia when she is living twenty yards away. We have the speed of technology to thank for that, I suppose. Thank goodness I don't have e-mail, or I could have known before she did!

She hasn't spoken to me since I confronted her with your letter, but Sabrina came back from school demanding a home computer, so I've had to communicate with Damon. He's as pleased as a pit bull terrier with two tails. He's already making a list of names and has started to call me Mother.

I hope this *doesn't* find you as it leaves me—hurt and confused.

Yours,

Irene . . . I mean Vera!

Saturday

Dear Howard,

I am writing to tell you, since I'm sure Karen won't—really, when I think of the money I've wasted on joined-up-writing tuition!—that we are to have an addition to the family. You will soon be the proud uncle of a boy called Dale or Liam or Vinny. I dread to think what the poor mite will be named if she's a girl, but Damon doesn't entertain the possibility.

I only found out by a chance remark from Irene. Proof, as ever, that Karen cuts me cruelly out of her life. It'll be a different story when she wants baby clothes or a baby-sitter.

Sorry, dear, if I'm sounding depressed. Sometimes I think the world has changed in such a bewildering way, I no longer feel a part of it.

Hope you and Antony are happy at least, with the sheep.

Mumsie

Dear Ms Matthews,

I understand from my granddaughter, Sabrina Small, that, to keep abreast of her studies, she must have a 'state-of-the-art' computer with built-in modem, fax and heliport. I am an OAP on an inadequate fixed income (has Tony Blair considered people like us in his enthusiasm for 'IT', I wonder?), and I'm at a loss to know where to turn. Are there any grants available?

Yours sincerely,

Vera Small

Thursday

Dear Vera,

I'm very worried about you—you seem
absolutely distraught! In fact you must be, to
send me all your other correspondence in your
last. I'm sending back the enc., because I don't
know Sabrina's school's address, but I've
forwarded Howard's letter on to him at
Sheepdipper's. I've also taken the liberty of
writing a little note to Karen, in the hope of
pouring oil on troubled waters.

Now come on, chin up, look at the
positive—I've been reading all about it in one
of Lesley's many self-help books that she
bought when she was going through the
divorce. You count your blessings—write them
down. You'll be surprised how they add up!

Oh dear, I was going to help by starting a
list, but it's time for tennis, so you'll have to do
it on your own. Probably more therapeutic,
anyway.

Cheerio for now, and get on with that list!

Sending love and encouraging thoughts,

Irene xx

19 Byron Street
St Urban
Melbourne

Thursday

Dear Howard,

Your mother sent the enc. to me in error, so
by the time you get this, what with the post,
she'll have been waiting a couple of weeks for
a reply. She seems in a terrible state, and I
really think she needs a break from trailer
park life. Couldn't you and Antony have her to
stay for a little holiday? I know she can be
difficult, but I do think it sounds like a real cry
for help, don't you? Would you let me know
how she seems when you see her?

Fondest regards, and also to Antony,

Irene Spencer

Thursday

Dear Karen,

Here at last are the bootees I promised. I made them in unisex yellow, as you can see. I told your Mum about the baby, as you asked, and you were right—it did come as a bit of a shock, but I'm sure inside she's as thrilled as you are. I think it might have helped if you'd told her that you and Damon were an 'item', as you call it, from the start. I think she thought of him as *her* special friend—she often mentioned him in her letters—so there may have been a little bit of jealousy there. Just a thought.

Anyway, dear, I know you try to be kind and patient with her. And of course I don't think you were selfish to move out of the caravan and leave her on her own. I spent several weeks cooped up in a Dormobile with her when we toured the Continent, don't forget, and I thought I'd end up in the funny farm!

Take care, and love to Damon,

Lots of love and hugs,

Rene xxx

Wed.

Dear Irene,

Enjoying a few days at magical Middle Parks. It was Sabrina's half-term and what with everything I felt I needed a break, so I cashed in a little insurance policy and we just took off. Sabrina is having a fine old time with all the activities, and I am basking in the indoor 'sun', so much more reliable than the real thing and, I believe, less damaging. You would know all about that in Australia, of course—doesn't it hold the world record for skin cancer? Hope you are not economising with the sun block on your tennis outings. One looks a fool with all those white stripes, but better safe than sorry.

You've probably written in reply to my last so this may cross with it, but I just wanted to put your mind at rest that I'm feeling much better, what with the aromatherapy massage (Yasmin's instructions) and leisurely drinks round the pool. Just popped on a sarong—I'm sure you've discovered them, so comfortable— to go for one now. A charming widower here has invited me for 'tropical cocktails'.

I enclose a couple of postcards so you can see the luxuriant foliage.

Love, and thanks for being a good,
albeit distant, friend.

Vera

Dear Howard,

Just a quick postcard from our lovely residence. I never imagined a 'log cabin' could be so comfortable. A huge bath and no need to wrestle with gas cylinders. I could stay here for ever.

Sabrina sends love, as I do,

Mumsie

Very late on Saturday night

Dear Vera,

Thank you for the postcard. I'm so relieved you seem to be feeling better—I was quite worried about you. Depression is an awful thing, isn't it? Or so I suppose—I've never suffered from it myself, fortunately.

Since I last wrote I have joined a creative writing class for senior citizens. It's funny, isn't it? I have to come to the other side of the world to do things that I could have been doing all along at home—playing tennis, penning poems—but one just doesn't seem to get round to it in the normal run of things. I suppose it is that, knowing so few people here, there aren't the usual distractions. Apart from looking after Cheryl Marie full-time, that is. Lesley's had to go away for a week on a course now. Her boss seems to think a great deal of her. He came to pick her up personally in his car to run her out to the airport.

I can't seem to get to sleep tonight, so I've been having a bit of fun alone, opening up a few bottles of the Victorian wine Lesley bought me, and doing blind tastings. I don't know if I'm getting any better at it—they all seem to taste nice to me—but it passes the time.

Oh, well. I'll try to sleep again. At this rate, Cheryl Marie will be up before I've gone to bed!

Hope you are still feeling the benefit of your holiday,

Fond regards,

Irene

PS Couldn't sleep, so penned this poem, enc.:

Reflections in the Dead of Night

a poem by
Irene Spencer

Looking up at the coal-black sky,
I see my life, and wonder why—
Why did I do this, why did I do that,
E.g., why did I buy that hat?

It looked so pretty in the shop,
With bows a-quiver, brim a-flop—
What happened on the way back home
To change it to a shapeless dome?

And isn't that a lot like life,
When you cut it apart with the surgeon's
    knife,
How oft do we rush after new fool's gold,
Instead of treasuring the trusty old?

Lodge 202
Far Shores Trailer Park

Saturday

Irene!

Arrived home to crossed letters and crossed wires! What on earth did you say to Howard and Karen after my confidential disclosures? Whatever it was has released a maelstrom. Howard was convinced I had run away to live in a log cabin. It was a 'cry for help' and I was in a 'terrible state' as I am jealous of Karen's relationship with Damon. They all agreed I'd gone completely round the twist and absconded with Sabrina! I was lucky to escape arrest. They have had the police out scouring the country and hourly bulletins on National radio. It was only the peace and seclusion of Middle Piddle that kept me from knowing about it.

I have explained to the police that I left a note under the door of Damon's trailer, and his blasted pit bull terrier must have chewed it, but they refuse to believe me. They are now considering prosecution.

Judging by the doggerel you enclosed, I can only assume you got carried away by the 'creative' side of your writing. Either that or

81

you have been indulging in too many blind tastings. If this is what you call 'treasuring the trusty old' I'd rather not be one of them!

Karen is demanding I give Sabrina back, though she of course wants to stay with me, and I am now to be assessed by social workers. A Ms Clinch is coming to make a 'home visit'.

Don't write again unless it is to offer something in mitigating circumstances.

Vera

dear Auntie Vera,

Granny is cryin all the time and drinkin a lot of pop. I have dawred you this picsure of you lookin cross, and she has writ you a pome. She is very sorry.

Love from

Cheryl Marie xxxxxxxxxxxxxxx

Dear Vera,

The Judgement Of The Damned

A poem by
Irene Spencer

One day—alas, 'twill be all too soon—
I will stand in the line to be judged:
To one side will go the souls that are clean,
To the other, the souls that are smudged.

As I shuffle along on penitent knees,
My head bowed before me in shame,
I will know that St Peter will turn me away,
For 'twas I who was wholly to blame.

'What is your crime?' my Maker will say,
His voice sending ice down my spine,
'Will you be going along with Old Nick,
Or are you a daughter of Mine?'

'I have sinned, Lord,' I'll say in a trembling
   voice,
'And must go to the fires of Hell.'
'Let me be the judge,' He'll say in fierce

tone,
'Begin now, your story to tell.'

I'll tell Him of when I was far from home,
Of the letters that crossed on the sea,
Of the misunderstandings, the heartache I
   caused,
I will tell Him of Vera and me.

And when I am finished, the Lord's voice
   will lift
To Lucifer, Keeper of Hell,
'Forget it,' He'll say, 'she's coming with me,
For her "sin" was just loving too well.'

But alas that is fantasy, only a dream,
I am still in the state known as Life.
If only, my heart cries, my friend was like
   God,
Forgiving, and staying her knife.

I meant well, my friend, cannot mercy be
   mine?
Can I not make your heart feel a sway?
If sackcloth and ashes could undo the harm,
Dear Vera, I'd wear them each day.

With love from Irene (x?)

Far Shores Trailer Park

Monday

Dear Irene,

I was stunned by your recent missive. How long have you been having conversations with God? I showed it to my psychic next-door neighbour Yasmin, and she asked if you've ever thought of the 'laying on of hands'? I said that as far as I knew only on gullible widowers.

I don't know what to make of the sentiments expressed, but it's obvious to me that all this Australian wine-tasting you've spoken about has taken you over completely. If you really want help, get off the 'pop' and into the sackcloth and ashes.

Since you are on such intimate terms with God, *I* need you to intercede for *me*. Urgently. My fate is in His hands and your knees. The social worker, Ms Clinch, is paying her 'home visit' on Friday, and if we fail to live up to her expectations (whatever they may prove to be), she may take my granddaughter, Sabrina, away from me and give her back to her awful mother—or should I say, she who used to be known as my daughter, Karen?

Vera

86

PS In case God is deaf to your pleas, I have pinned up your verses to our notice-board. Hopefully they will frighten Ms Clinch into making the right decisions.

Tuesday

Dear Vera,

I hope you don't mind me calling you that. I
don't think we've ever met, but my Mum,
Irene, talks so much about you that I feel I
know you. I've been having to deal with her
mail recently, and your last note sounded
pretty urgent, so I thought I'd better reply.

Mum has been under a bit of strain lately
and I've had to admit her to a private clinic I
managed to find upstate. Nothing major, just a
little breakdown—you know how nervy she
can get. Maybe it's been too much for her
having to look after Cheryl Marie. I don't
know—you think you're doing her a favour,
making her feel needed, and then she pulls a
stunt like this. As it is, I had to take a couple of
days off work to sort everything out, and I've
hired an au pair, so when they let Mum out
she'll be able to go back home to England. I'll
let you know when that is, as I'm sure you'll
want to pick her up from the airport, you two
being such old friends.

I'll pass on your letter when I next visit her

if she's up to focusing again, but they thought it might take a little while for the hallucinations to stop, so personally I'm not holding my breath.

All the best,

Lesley Crabtree, née Spencer

Lodge 202
Far Shores Trailer Park

Saturday

Dear Lesley,

How nice to have personal contact with you at last after all this time. Of course, I feel I know you well . . . too well on occasions . . . from all your mother's comments. But I'm sure in real life you are very different. Actually, we did meet once, at your wedding. You looked magical in your Princess Di frock, all pink and giggly. You may not remember, you were quite tipsy from the wine—I understand from Irene you have a lot of it in Oz, so I hope you still enjoy it as much as she does. Anyway, it was a lovely occasion, though perhaps, under the circumstances, you won't wish to be reminded. It's so sad when marriages break up. Your mother gave me a blow-by-blow account of yours. All your psychiatric treatment and chanting and self-help manuals! I know she was very concerned for you.

Speaking of which, I'm so sorry to hear about Irene. Whatever is the matter? Hallucinations?! I must admit, looking back, her last few letters were rather odd. Positively unhinged, in fact, especially the last one. Full

90

of wild 'poetic' ramblings. I understand some poets *are* prone to hallucinations—Samuel Taylor Coleridge, for example—but at least he wrote reasonable rhymes when under the influence. Your mother's efforts would have disgraced a Christmas cracker. In a way, it's a relief to know she was 'on' something.

I blame myself, of course. I should have paid more attention. Friends can tell each other things they'd never admit to their daughters, and she might have confided her 'problem'. Where I wonder did she get hold of the 'substances'? Surely not at the tennis club?! Here, it would be no problem. A trailer park is like a pharmacy, except it doesn't stock hot-water bottles.

I've been having my own troubles with Health. In this case, Environmental. I won't bore you with the details—it's all to do with the suitability of my home for my own dear little granddaughter, Sabrina. Really, four fire extinguishers in fifteen square feet should be enough, but no—it's fireproof doors and fireproof sheets . . . It's not as though Sabrina or I smoke in bed! A rather unpleasant Ms Clinch descended with her stormtroopers and stripped the place, looking for goodness knows what. They went through Sabrina's hair for nits, made a list of the contents of the fridge and took a sample for 'analysis' from the toilet! You'd think that if a child was well fed, clean, happy and loved it would be enough, but not, it seems, compared to the contents of the Elsan. I haven't heard their decision yet, and I must say I'm living on the edge of an abyss. And I'm not talking about the Elsan.

Don't give Irene my last note—it might push *her* into one. I'm enclosing another, and a postal order for flowers—something pastel—which I'm sure you'll be kind enough to purchase. Do let me know how she goes on.

Best regards,

Vera

Dear Irene,

I am sorry to hear about your breakdown. Has God been appearing to you again? Or was it a 'contretemps' with your boyfriend, Vincent? I never felt right about him. He was altogether too good to be true. Especially the teeth. Anyone of that age who tells you they are his own is either a freak of nature or lying.

Lesley tells me you are coming home to England, and to be honest I'm glad. Australia's too far away, and, by the sound of it, dangerous. You will be fine once you are back. At least English madness is familiar.

Do write as soon as you can tell a pen from a knife.

All my love,

Vera

PS My psychic neighbour Yasmin says try to record your 'hallucinations'.

Room 101
Woolabulla WellBeing Clinic
Woolabulla

Dear Vera,

I am sneaking this out with someone who's leaving. Please come and rescue me. I'm sure I shouldn't be in here—everybody is mad. A woman with a nasty face has visited me once, claiming to be my daughter. She brought me some bright pink and purple flowers that looked like ladies' unmentionables, and your note. Who is she—is she one of Them? They give me pills that make me feel funny, and one time tried to toast my head in a machine. I'm not sure how long I've been here, but I think it could be about ten years.

I am sending hallucinations for Yasmin in blank poetry form (thankfully we have Creative Writing Therapy here)—I hope she enjoys them better than me. The drugs trolley is coming!!!! I've got to hide.

I'll expect you tomorrow. Bring wine.

Love,

Irene

PS Who is Vincent? Is he one of Them too?

Hallucinations for Yasmin

by
I. Spencer

Yellow men with funny fingers
Purple polyps on my nose
Frilly fringes in my eyebrow
Wires and spikes and all things nice
Rats as big as full moon craters
Leaving dentures on my bed
Howling winds and grinning mices
The cork's in the bottle!
The cork's in the bottle!
The cork's in the bottle and it can't get out!!!!!

Friday

Dear Lesley,

I received the most barmy note from Irene (enc.). I showed it to my next-door neighbour Yasmin, a trained psychic, and she said it's obvious Irene is on Planet Zog. I don't know where that is, but if the hallucinations are anything to go by it must be very unpleasant.

I am now seriously worried about her condition. I only wish I could come and get her, but I'm up to my neck in plasterboard— all the fault of the Environmental Dept— they've got a cheek, calling themselves 'Health'.

I feel I should warn you, she seems to have taken against you. Do be careful. She can be very aggressive, as I know to my cost. There's only one way to deal with her when she gets like this!

Fond regards,

Vera

Dear Irene,

Pull yourself together. You're behaving like a loony. In fact, you are a loony. Never mind the pills—if you carry on like this 'They' will have you in a strait-jacket. Believe me, I know. The number of times Karen's tried to have me Sectioned! In case you've forgotten, Karen is my daughter and your friend. I have asked her to write to you.

Looking back over our recent correspondence, it occurs to me your troubles all come from the bottom of a glass. Many bottoms. You, Irene, are an alcoholic. There, I've said it.

Take the medication! It will return you to normal. Well, as normal as can be expected. I'm sure you're hiding it in very inventive places. I haven't forgotten how cunning you were, when you fell out with my cooking.

Try and focus on the good things in your life. Apart from wine, that is. Above all, keep the cork in the bottle!

Tough love,

Vera

PS I am enclosing a note from my psychic neighbour Yasmin.

97

Running Water Lodge
Far Shores Trailer Park

Dear Irene,

I feel a ruby-red aura around you, which is causing the distress. I shall send absent healing. Meanwhile, meditate on the crystal enclosed and try rubbing it on the polyps.

Yours in spirit,

Yasmin Brown
(spells, tarot and psychic counselling)

Dear Vera,

Thanks for your letter of a few weeks ago and sorry I haven't replied sooner. The au pair I told you about proved to be a disaster, and I've had to take loads of time off work to look after my daughter, Cheryl Marie, myself.

I hope you don't mind, but I read the note you sent Mum. The alcoholic bit made a lot of sense to me—she drained a dozen bottles of wine I bought her for her birthday in a couple of days. Told me she'd spilt them! Anyway, it scemed to make sense to her too when she read it, and although it made her very upset at first, soon afterwards she seemed to pull herself together and make steady progress, which the Clinic were very pleased with. Until this latest bombshell happened.

The Clinic phoned last night to tell me Mum has gone missing. Apparently, a woman calling herself Karen turned up, claiming to be 'Irene's friend Vera's daughter'. She had a man with her that the manager described as a 'gorilla', called Damon, who wouldn't take no for an answer, so they were allowed in to visit her. The next thing the staff at the Clinic knew

99

was that they had disappeared, apparently taking Mum with them. I don't mind—it was costing an arm and a leg to keep her in there, and apparently they were going to discharge her today anyway, but I just thought you should know.

Since I imagine they'll be taking her back to England, I've packed up the rest of Mum's things and shall be having them shipped across later in the week to her home address. Unfortunately, it's most of her clothes, and it'll take a couple of months to arrive, what with Customs checks in both countries. Anyway, if you hear from her before I do, will you tell her they're on their way?

Thanks for your help,

Irene's daughter, Lesley

The Outback

Thursday or Friday of this week

Dear Vera,

I'm free! Your daughter and son-in-law-to-be are my heroes! Feeling so much better, and am off the booze. Thank you for bringing me to my senses, old friend. Am still taking the tablets, which Karen managed to find in the clinic drugs trolley in a bottle labelled 'Irene Spencer'—talk about a coincidence! Anyway, they make me a bit tired and not quite sure of the date (see above)—but at least now I'm getting the week right!

Please thank your friend Yasmin for the absent healing, which seems to have worked a treat. I didn't know what to do with the crystal though—I've never had a polyp in my life, purple or otherwise.

Shall be coming home soon, but Damon said we should lie low for a while in case they've staked out the airports—sounds a bit paranoid to me! Still, he seems to know his way round a billycan, so we're living well, if rough. Karen is well. She's *so* pregnant and huge that we tell her she looks like the kangaroos, which at the moment are our nearest neighbours!

See you soon, I hope.
One step at a time.
I am an alcoholic . . . There, I've said it too!

Lots of love,

Irene

Saturday

Dear Lesley,

I am sorry to trouble you again, especially at a time when you're trying to find your feet as a mother, but I wonder if you've heard from Irene yet? I've had these last two letters (enc.) returned to me as 'Not known at this address'. Of course, 'The Outback, Australia', which is where she last wrote from, isn't much to go on. I'm so angry with my daughter, Karen, and her boyfriend, Damon. It's typical of their irresponsible behaviour, though they've never gone as far as abduction before. If you had all her clothes, whatever is Irene wearing? Surely she's not running round the bush in a hospital nightgown? And I dread to think what 'medication' they've got her on. Damon is probably growing it!

They left me in a terrible mess. Damon was half-way through building an extension to my trailer. I had to call in Dave from next-door-but-one, and he was horrified. Took the whole thing down and started again. Said it was an accident waiting to happen, could have caved in at any moment. Irene mentioned they are

103

'living rough'. I only hope Damon isn't exercising his so-called building skills, or they may not live long enough for me to see my new grandchild.

It's a pity you aren't enjoying motherhood more. Personally, I'm loving it. The only good thing about their disappearance is that the head social worker, Ms Clinch, is letting my granddaughter, Sabrina, stay with me. I've also got custody of Damon's Range Rover and his pit bull terrier. Fortunately, the extension is now finished!

Do forward the enc's if you can.

All best wishes,

Vera

Definitely Wednesday

Dear Irene,

Clearly you have not 'come to your senses' at all. What on earth are you doing living rough at your age? To say nothing of being a fugitive. Are you sure you got the right medication off that drugs trolley at the Clinic? It certainly doesn't sound like it.

For goodness' sake come home. You are behaving very selfishly, which of course is the mark of an alcoholic. I'm sure Lesley is very worried about you—when she has a moment between being a full-time mother and a full time estate agent. I certainly am. I wouldn't trust a dog to the care of those two. In fact, our social worker, Ms Clinch, confided she'd been on to the RSPCA about the pit bull terrier.

Yours,

Vera

PS Just remember, 'I am an alcoholic.'

PPS Damon *is* paranoid as a result of the medication *he's* on. I don't advise you to try it.

PPPS Nearly forgot. Please give Karen the enc. from social services.

Social Services
The Old Armoury
Grimm Street
Vicker-upon-St Agnes

Tuesday 18th

Dear Ms Karen Smalls,

I write to inform you that we are awarding temporary custody of your daughter, Sabrina Smalls, to Mrs Vera Smalls, her grandmother. We have taken all factors into account, including your contention of mental abuse in your childhood—though frankly, we don't usually see 'bursting into the bathroom when I was on the lavatory' as an abuse issue.

Your recent abandonment of your child has left us no other option.

Yours sincerely

Christobel Clinch
Social worker

Kookaburra's Rest
Lirralirra Falls
Australia

Thank God it's Friday

Dear Vera,

So much has happened here since I last wrote I hardly know where to start. I began to feel much more clear-headed when Damon confiscated my medication shortly after I wrote and started to take it himself. Unfortunately he grew even odder and rather aggressive. He thought Karen was a dingo and that she had swallowed her own baby, and kept pointing to her pregnant belly and shouting, 'Why's she so fat then, you tell me that?!' It was very upsetting and has made me do a complete rethink about my stance on banning sex education in schools. At least they could tell them that babies come out of ladies' tummies.

Anyway, Karen and I were so frightened that I decided to call my daughter, Lesley, to see if we could go there for a while. Apart from anything else, I only had the clothes I stood up in, and they were pretty grubby to say the least. She told us where to go (see above address), and to stay there till she arrived,

108

which is what we are doing. It's a lovely little guesthouse, and it seems they know Lesley here quite well. They say she often comes to stay here with a gentleman friend, but I'm sure they must have got that wrong.

She also read me the letters you sent. Karen was very angry about you getting custody of Sabrina—she said she asked you to take care of her for a while, while she came to rescue me, so what's all the fuss about? Then she found the note that she thought she'd left you, in her handbag, so now she doesn't blame you quite as much. I hope that the two of you manage to reconcile your differences—she's all for you doing family therapy together when she returns. I know for a fact that she still has recurring nightmares about the lavatory incidents the social worker dismissed so lightly.

I think we'll stay at Lesley's for a while, just to catch our breath, and then fly home in a couple of weeks, so if you're writing, please send letters there.

All for now, love

Irene

PS I think the drugs they gave me in the clinic made me a bit forgetful. I had no idea you were an alcoholic! I'm so sorry for you. I think they say, 'One step at a time,' don't they? Please try not to give in to temptation, particularly now you have become a temporary mother to your granddaughter.

Lodge 202 / 203
Far Shores Trailer Park

Sunday

Dear Irene,

The drugs must have addled your brain completely if you've forgotten *you* are the alcoholic! If you imagine the occasional sweet sherry is at all the same thing then you are much mistaken. I may have had one too many at the odd occasion—a wedding or a funeral, let's say—but I have never been through a crate on my own. There is absolutely no comparison. As if I would endanger the life of my dear little daughter—I mean *grand*daughter. You may wish to tell Karen, by the way, that Sabrina is fine and doesn't miss her at all. Well, why should she? She tells me Karen used to bribe her to stay under the bed when one of her unsuitable men came round. The things that child has seen! Karen is someone to complain about lavatory incidents. It looks as though Damon follows the pattern. Perhaps, now you have had a close encounter yourself, you are more inclined to believe me.

Here, Sabrina has my undivided attention. Apart from the dog. We've just come back from a lovely walk on the beach—he's covered

111

in seaweed! Of course we have to poop-and-scoop and stop him savaging toddlers, but he seems happier, poor thing. We paddled and skimmed stones and now we're playing on Sabrina's computer. (Yasmin got one from the cash and carry.) My favourite game is 'Helicopter GunChix'! Lots of girls in camouflage blasting all the baddies. Sabrina says she's going to be one when she grows up. And to think I wanted to be a librarian.

Let me know if and when you are returning and I will meet you with the Range Rover. I suppose I can do no less. You *are* my best friend, and Karen *is* my daughter.

I'll keep my fingers crossed for a speedy return of your memory.

All best wishes,

Vera

Lodge 202 / 203
Far Shores Trailer Park

Sunday

Dear Lesley,

I can't express how sorry I am you've been landed with both Irene and Karen. Let's hope Damon doesn't turn up as well—he can be very violent. Normally it's worse when he's taking drugs, and I understand from Irene he's currently taking her tablets from the Clinic. Heaven knows what they are.

If there is anything I can do to help, short of having them back here, do let me know.

Fond regards and good luck!

Vera

Dear Vera,

Here we are at Lesley's, safe and sound, so got your last, at last. I haven't told Karen any of the hurtful things you asked me to pass on, except to say that you are keeping her daughter Sabrina safe and well.

So far we've had no trouble from Damon since we escaped his clutches, although the television news is full of a 'Mystery Dingo Man' wandering around in the area of the bush where we last saw him, which could be him. If it is, he has apparently joined a pack of dingoes and is walking on all fours, and, if the artists' impressions are to be believed, has grown even more hirsute than usual.

Many things have become much clearer for me, and I have to say that your Karen has been a boon in that regard. She's explained things to me that I have obviously led too sheltered an existence to even dream of.

I think I do remember being a bit depressed, and yes—drinking a little too much—although where you get the idea I am an alcoholic I'll go to my grave never knowing. I was so very lonely. I'd travelled half-way round the world to see my daughter, and most of the time she was out. Of course it was lovely being able to be with my granddaughter, Cheryl Marie, every day, but there is only so much meaningful conversation you can have with a little girl her age. Australia is so very far away from everywhere, and I started to feel a bit stranded and hopeless, and wondering what I could possibly do to make my life better. All I could come up with was 'Nothing'. Actually, that wasn't quite all I could come up with. I also invented a nice story for myself to cheer myself up, about a man called Vincent. He did exist—still does, as far as I'm aware—but I exaggerated the depth of our relationship a little bit. In fact, our only contact was pairing each other in serve-and-volley practice on one occasion. I also gave him rather more hair and teeth in my fantasy than he actually possesses in real life. But I digress.

I remember hitting a case of wine that Lesley had bought me rather hard one night, and then realising to my horror that I was drunk and incapable and in charge of a minor—Lesley was out as usual, and as usual I was baby-sitting. I felt very ashamed of myself, not to mention extremely giddy and horribly nauseous. I put myself under a cold shower and started to feel a little more clear-headed, and then I remembered some special herbal tea I had seen Lesley taking at night-time which she keeps in a caddy in her smalls drawer. When I'd asked her what it was, she'd said it helped to calm her down and get things in perspective, so naturally I thought it might be just the thing to sober me up. I put the kettle on, and given how much I needed to get things in perspective, put two spoonfuls in for me, and three for the pot.

Vera, you'll never guess in a million years what Karen now tells me it was! Illegal drugs! Something called maryjuana—have you heard of it? According to her, I took enough of the stuff to send me right off what remained of my rocker!

Naturally I have told Lesley off now in no uncertain terms about taking drugs, although both she and Karen tell me I'm making a fuss about nothing. They say that even the Home Secretary has admitted to taking it when he was a student, although apparently he doesn't admit to inhaling. Frankly I don't know what difference that makes—I mean, who would inhale when they're drinking tea?

Anyway, she's promised me she won't do it again, so I suppose some good has come out of it. Another piece of nice news is that our daughters seem to be following in our footsteps and have become almost inseparable pals. Even now as I write they are holed up in Lesley's bedroom together having a really good girls' night in—I can hear their merry giggles from out here on the veranda! Not that I feel left out.

Well, all for now. I'm still very tired and keep needing to catch up on my sleep, but I wanted to put your mind at rest that all is as well as can be expected, and that Karen and I will be staying on here for a while longer.

Lots of love,

Irene

Dear Irene,

Fond of you as I am, I would never describe us as 'inseparable'. In my opinion we are at our best with several thousand miles between us. However, I am very glad to hear you seem to have regained your wits and can now tell the difference between herbal tea and mind-altering substances. Incidentally, next time you feel the need to gain perspective, or 'chill out' in trailer-park parlance, you might try two drops of lavender oil and a candle in the bath (Yasmin's recipe), a sheep's yoghurt massage (my son Howard's) or Horlicks, a hot-water bottle and a good book (mine).

I'm glad the 'girls' are getting on so well. Perhaps Lesley (who seems so affectionate) will teach Karen some manners. I'm a little concerned about the giggling—are you sure you threw away the rest of the marijuana? In my experience of addicts (everyone in the trailer-park, including the children), just saying 'no' is not an option. I know for a fact that Karen and Damon smoked home-grown 'grass', as they call it, every day. Trust Karen. And when she's pregnant as well. The baby will certainly have green fingers—at this rate it

118

will be lucky to escape a green head. Is she intending to have it there, by the way? In which case it will be Australian. Appropriate enough, I suppose, since its father is a dingo.

Well, on to more pleasant topics. Sabrina and I are planting a garden round the trailer. It's too late for it to bloom this year, of course, but it should be lovely for the Spring. If we are still here, that is. Social Services are considering rehousing us. Ms Clinch is not happy with the company Sabrina keeps (see above)—something about 'peer pressure'. Though I must say, whatever their problems, Yasmin's children are charming. They've just been round with some seedlings for us to plant in the window boxes.

Whoops—I can see scuds of earth flying past the window. The dog is digging. We've renamed him 'Rex' after Tyrannosaurus, since, depending on how much grass he had smoked, Damon used to call him 'Ronnie' or 'Reg'. No wonder the poor thing is violent. I'd better go and rescue my poor plants!

All for now.

My love to you,

Vera

PS Please pass the enclosed letter on to Karen.

Dear Karen,

I have spoken to Ms Clinch about your family therapy idea. To be honest she doesn't hold out much hope for us, but I am willing to try if you are. Anything, if it will make you less rude, judgemental and unloving. Then again, perhaps since you're having such a good time, you will stay in Australia.

I enclose some paintings Sabrina did for you at school. Don't be alarmed by the female figures being stabbed and set on fire. According to her teacher, it's healthy for Sabrina to express her 'matricidal anger'.

We both look forward to hearing about the baby. What a pity you won't have a partner at your side. You'd better teach Irene 'Ten Green Bottles'. Though come to think of it, that's the last thing she should be singing.

Your loving Mother

St Urban
Melbourne
Australia

Dear Vera,

Or should I say, Dear Granny? Glad tidings and great joy, for unto you a grandson is born! Mother and baby are now doing well and came back home today. It's amazing, isn't it, the way they turf them out of hospital so quickly nowadays, when we were cosseted and kept in cotton wool in nursing homes for a fortnight. Karen's labour, poor thing, was as long and gruelling as it was sudden and unexpected. According to her calculations, it wasn't due for another two months, but here he is, a bonny eight and a half pounds, and apparently fully formed. The hospital certainly seem to think he is a full-term baby. It's made me wonder quietly to myself if Damon could be the father. How long has she known him? It can't be nine months already, can it?

Certainly there is no trace of Damon in his looks, you'll be relieved to know. He has a much higher forehead, for a start, and what there is so far of his hair is a beautiful golden colour. He has long legs and very refined hands, and a look of intelligence in his eyes that I have never noticed in Damon. Best of all, as far as you're concerned, is that you have another grandchild born with your very distinctive nose, so there's certainly no mix-up as to who his grandmother is!

All for now as I'm supposed to be washing nappies. Karen is very Eco, isn't she? She says it would take a forest the size of Sherwood to provide enough raw materials to keep him in disposables until he's potty-trained, and she has more respect for the planet than that. Just goes to show we weren't wrong about everything when we were young mums!

I've taken some photos of mother and son and will send them when they're developed, in my next. No name for the little chap yet, as Karen wants to get to know his personality first. She has a theory that wrong naming can cripple a child's development. Apparently she's always seen herself as being more of a Cassandra than a Karen. She would also like his lineage to be reflected in his second and third names, and asks to be reminded of the names of her two grandfathers. Can you let us know?

Congratulations, Granny Small!

More soon,

With love,

Nanny Spencer!!

Lodge 202 / 203
Far Shores Trailer Park

Dear Irene,

Sorry about the delay in responding. Life on the trailer park has been even more dramatic than usual. Yasmin was hard up, so she dumped her kids with me and went to Amsterdam for a few days. Apparently they are very keen on her massages over there and give her a lovely little booth with curtains and a pink light, which she says is marvellous for relaxation. She returned to find her trailer had been completely ransacked! Everything had gone, including her stock of essential oils, which was disastrous as she'd completely run out—she'd had such a busy time with them. We didn't hear a thing, but of course one gets used to the nightly screams, shouts and crashes. Once my sponge earplugs are in I could sleep through a chainsaw massacre! The police have refused to investigate, as the park is a 'no-go' area, but Site Security, who are always informed when people go away, say that there has been a spate of raids and we're the victims of a serial ransacker. I must talk to Dave-next-door-but-one about getting iron bars for the windows.

Naturally we are delighted that Karen has

been safely delivered. I'm not surprised her labour took so long. After breaking my waters two weeks early at a Masonic dinner dance, she took the rest of the fortnight to arrive. By the time she was born I was crawling round the floor begging to be put out of my misery.

The father of the new baby is as much a mystery to me as it probably is to her. I have no idea what she got up to before she met Damon. Sabrina remembers a tall blond man who visited Howard at Sheepdipper's. She thinks he was the vet. I didn't like to probe— she's only six—but she says he and Karen often went to the sheep shed together. Someone has to hold the sheep's head while the vet shoves his hand up the other end, so perhaps one thing led to another. But I'd be amazed if it's any friend of Howard's—as far as I know, they are all of the 'other persuasion'.

Please give Karen the enclosed card and baby-grow. I got one with the longest legs, so I hope it will accommodate. Sabrina is really looking forward to seeing the pictures of her little brother. As to names, Karen's paternal grandfather was called Wilfred, but he was rather unpleasant. Karen never liked sitting on his knee. My father was a Charlie. Sabrina suggests 'Robbie', after her favourite pop star.

Must finish and cook tea for all the kids and Yasmin. I'm feeding them until Yasmin gets a new cooker installed. It's a good job she did so

124

well in Amsterdam. She insists she loves her work, but I must say she looks knackered.

Love to you all and a kiss for my new grandson. It's getting to be quite a tribe!

Vera

PS It appears I *did* sleep through a chainsaw massacre. Security tell me there was one the other night at Trailer 206. A 'domestic' that got out of hand. The trailer's just a pile of splintered wood and there were no survivors.

Dear Vera,

Here at last are the photographs of 'Baby Boy Small'—still no name yet, so we're calling him by the name that was on his hospital armband. Makes him sound like a boxer, doesn't it?! Sorry the pictures are a bit blurred, but I was trembling with nerves trying to use the new camera I'd treated myself to. It says it's fully automatic on the box, and then when you get it home you find it's like a computer, full of digital whatsits and 'menus', whatever they are. So far I haven't found anything on one that you would want to eat. Anyway, as you see, I had to put it on the 'Panamaric Menu' so we could get the full length of his legs in. Isn't he bonny?! I'm glad at least that his nose is in focus, so you can see for yourself how it runs in the family.

I am so sorry to hear of the level of violence and civil unrest at Far Shores Trailer Park. No wonder your social worker Ms Clinch wants to get you moved. Any joy yet? When I mentioned it to Karen she gave what we used to call an 'old-fashioned look', and

126

recommends that you don't ever tell Site Security when you're going away. She says that when Damon was working for them they used to take it as a *carte blanche* for going in and helping themselves to people's possessions. She also said that if you look inside the Range Rover's inner mysteries, you will see that something called the 'shassy' number has been filed off. Of course, it could just be a filament of her over-active imagination, but maybe you'd better check—you could be found guilty of driving stolen goods. Perhaps Dave-next-door-but-one could help you identify the 'shassy'—I'm afraid I've no idea what one is.

Karen is doing well *'post partum'*, and in fact has expressed some of her milk so that I can feed Baby Boy tonight while she and Lesley go for a 'girls' night out'. I must say she's recovered her figure quickly, judging by her costume choice when they left!

Anyway, mustn't luxuriate too long in the world of words—Nanny Spencer is on full time duty tonight! Plus I am having to run myself up a few frocks since apparently Lesley mistakenly sent all my clothes back to England. Could you send me that Butterick pattern you used to have for the box-pleated summer frock, if you still have it to hand? I know it's old, but it always looked so timeless on you.

Baby Boy sends a kiss to his Granny Small

and to his sister Sabrina.

                Love,

                Irene

Dear Irene,

Thank you for your newsy letter and the photos of the baby. Or rather, his nose. It looks like a trunk. I can see no resemblance to mine at all. And those legs certainly don't come from my side of the family. Baby Boy 'Small' seems most inappropriate. Sabrina was terribly disappointed—she of course is so petite and her nose is a little button—much more like Granny's. We both think it's time he had a proper name, whatever nonsense Karen spouts about his 'personality'. At this rate he will grow up without one. Sabrina took another look at the pictures and suggested 'Gabby' after her goldfish. Though to be honest, 'Gummy' would be nearer the mark. I hope you've mastered the camera by the next set. Are you sure the shaking hands were due to nerves, and not one too many 'you-know-whats'? I'm sorry if that sounds blunt but, as a true friend, I consider it my duty to be vigilant.

I *do* know what you mean about technology. Yasmin has finally got her new digi-cooker installed and I have been trying to use it. (Yasmin, poor love, has had to take a night job.) It's got hundreds of labour-saving devices, but a 'menu'—which in the case of a cooker you might expect—is the last thing I can find. I can't even get the blasted gas to light. The children have had to have sandwiches for the last few days. I've telephoned British Gas a dozen times, but all I get is Vivaldi. That poor man must be turning in his grave at what they've done to his 'Four Seasons'!

I've also had to forbid Sabrina access to the 'net'. She kept trying to download pornography. It's the influence of Yasmin's kids, I'm afraid. They whizz about all over the place on it. Sometimes it's hard to tell if they're playing violent techno-games or watching worldwide atrocities. Speaking of which, Ms Clinch brought some charming refugees to view the trailer. They liked it much better than the converted lavatory they'd been camping in and weren't a bit put off by the murder and mayhem on the site. They said they'd been living with that for years in Kosovo. I'm keeping my fingers crossed, though the trailer, even with extension, is a little small for ten of them.

Must stop—it's time to wrestle with the cooker again. Where will it all end? Trust men to do away with God and put a microchip in his place. It will serve them right if everything does collapse on 1st Jan. 2000! I suppose we women, as usual, will have to pick up the pieces. And make the sandwiches.

My love as ever,

Vee

PS Almost forgot. Looked everywhere for that Butterick pattern, but no joy. I threw masses away when I moved here—as I'm sure I've mentioned, space is limited. I'm sending the frock instead. I haven't worn it for years. I'm sure you can let it out in the right places.

PPS Dave-next-door-but-one is in bed with his back, so I asked Terry-who-makes-the-sex-videos about the 'shassy'. He laughed and said the only one he'd ever laid a finger on was Carol's. Given the nature of their 'work', I didn't inquire further.

Dear Vera,

Thank you for the frock, which I've managed to take in after battling for long hours with the thirty-six box pleats. In order to get it to fit me (being petite) I've had to reduce it to twenty-four pleats while letting out the bust a little. Quite a job! In fact I'd have been quicker if I'd woven the material myself before making it! However, since it was so voluminous in the skirt, I had enough material left over to make a little frock for Cheryl Marie and a tiny little top for Baby Boy. You can imagine, we cut quite a dash when we go shopping together in them, which we did today. One old lady with whom we queued for vegetables at the market said we reminded her of the Beverley Sisters! I haven't thought of them for years, have you? They were so wonderful, and such beautiful '*chanteuses*', and such a nice picture of 'family', don't you think? It's such a pity that the young don't have such clean-cut, normal, effervacious role models any more, isn't it? It's no wonder Yasmin's children run a bit wild when the pop heroes are called things like 'Beastie Boys' these days. If only Sir Cliff Richard was still top of the pops—it would be such a different story.

Which brings me to your good deeds. Vera, are you sure you aren't biting off more than you can chew by offering a home to those refugees? It is so kind of you, but surely, when you had the extension built, it was so that you and Sabrina had more room for yourselves, not so you could become another branch of the Red Cross? Where on earth will you all sleep? Surely you are already doing enough for the community by feeding a prostitute's children? Which of course is very Christian of you, but then again it would be, wouldn't it? Jesus himself was our generation's role model. In fact if it hadn't been for Sunday School and lessons about Mary Magdalene, I probably would still be none the wiser about 'the oldest profession'.

It is the weekend here—well, come to think of it, I suppose it is the weekend there, but when you're so far away it's difficult to imagine things happening at the same time—and Lesley has taken Karen away to Kookaburra's Rest to 'chill out', which I believe is what they say these days instead of 'to relax'. Kookaburra's Rest, upstate in Lirralirra, was where we stayed, you may remember, when we ran away from Damon after he had decided he was a dingo. There has been some dramatic and tragic news of him, which is why Karen needs to be 'chilled out'—newspaper cutting enc. She is debating whether to help police with their inquiries, but I think she will prefer to keep silent. She doesn't want Baby Boy to be tainted with a lurid past by the gutter press, and I can't say I blame her.

Anyway, mustn't stop. Nappies to wash, entertainment for Cheryl Marie to be organised, babies to be bathed! The fridge is full to bursting with expressed milk—Karen said she felt like a Friesian cow before she left! I feel as if I could do with 'chilling out' myself, to be absolutely honest!

Take care, and do think about what I said about giving too much to others.

With love,

Irene

PS Just a thought—apropos of Yasmin's digi-cooker—could it be possible that you can't light the gas because it's electric?

PPS 'A slab of tinnies' is a case of lager, I believe, and a chook is a chicken—see news cutting.

'I SAVED AUSTRALIA FROM THE DINGO MAN AND NOW I'M BEING PUNISHED!'

An Eyewitness Account as told to *Digger* Reporter
Stu Jackson

PETE DALEWOOD **is a good bloke. Everybody what knows him says so. And so's his wife Bev. They don't lie, they can handle a couple of slabs of tinnies apiece, and both of them are bloody good shots. A perfect pair of Ockers, you might say, but that's where you'd be wrong, according to whingeing sissy liberal police chief Franco Bianchi.**

A dab hand with the rifle, and a keen reader of our sister magazine *Gotcha!*, Pete was shooting a few dingo vermin while posing for Bev's amature photos what they hoped would get printed in 'Readers' Pickies' in the mag next month. Bang! Crack! Bull's-eye! Another dingo falls to Pete's top gun!! But when they stroll over to inspect the shot patterns, instead of a dingo there's a hairy bloke turned belly up, dead as a doornail and ten times as bloody.

'Bev and me was minding our own business,' says Pete today from his police cell, 'taking a few shots at some dingoes what were killing our chooks. What's a bloke supposed to do, for Christ's sake? Let 'em eat your chooks and turn the other cheek? How was I supposed to know at that distance that one of em was a human being? 'Sides, everybody knows that Dingo Man's been terrorising the whole of Australia. If I had him in my sights right now, I'd do the same thing again. What's happen-ing to this bloody country? In other places in the world, I'd be a hero, not a crim.'

Now we can all sleep safe in our beds at night, Pete is being charged with murder, and the little lady is grieving at home alone. 'It's that bloody poofter anti-gun lobby,' says Bev, a blonde beauty. 'They've got that wog Bianchi by the short and curlies. Pete done good, and look where it got him. I'm starting a campaign, and anybody what wants to join up can turn up at the demo tomorrow. I am standing by my man. He's a hero. That Dingo Man is now where he belongs – in hell. And I know a few other people what ought to be joining him!'

The Dingo Man's identity is still a mystery, but as readers will see from Bev's superb close-ups on pages 3 and 4, the tattoos 'Rule Britannia' and 'Arsenal for Ever' tell their own tale. 'If Poms want to come here and get back to nature,' says Pete, 'that's their business. But now they know what happens to 'em if they do.'

Vera and Sabrina and Rex have moved to a new home!

New Address:

Flat 2
19-23 Mandela Court
Thrush Grove
Vicker-upon-St Agnes

Dear Irene,

No room on this postcard for more than a quick hello! Ms Clinch came up trumps. Apart from some strange fungicidal growth in the crevices, this s/c, two bdrm, all elec., digi-free council flt with pkg and gdn is delightful. I must say it's a relief to be off the trailer park. The chainsaw incident was the last straw—or perhaps I should say 'splinter'. I do hope the refugees will be all right there. I understand they are Muslim, so I left them the mats and a rack full of vegetables. I drew the line at Halal chicken, though I'm sure the chainsaw wielder would have obliged.

More as soon as we are settled,

Vee

PS Am writing to Howard to try to find out if Baby Boy's possible father, the vet, is still around.

Dear Howard,

A quick note with my new address. The council finally rehoused us. You may like to know, as I'm sure Karen won't have informed you, that you now have a large Australian nephew known as 'Baby Boy Small'. His father—as far as we know—has been shot dead whilst masquerading as a dingo (it's a long story—don't ask), so he, like Sabrina, will grow up without one. Perhaps, under the circumstances, that is a blessing. I don't think a dingo is the best role model. Do you, by any chance, still have that nice vet? You might like to mention Karen's news to him.

Will stop now. Busy with decorating. When we arrived everything was red, green and gold!

Mumsie

St Urban
Melbourne
Australia

Dear Vee and Sabrina,

Welcome to your new home! I am delighted to hear you have escaped the trailer park, and wish you certain happiness and peace in Mandela Court. You may be surprised to know that its good influence has already made its mark 'Down Under'—when I showed your postcard to Karen and she saw your new address, she was inspired to finally name Baby Boy. A big welcome then, please, for Nelson Wilfred Charlie St John Small! (The first two middle names are for his great-grandparents, of course, but I don't know who is responsible for the 'St John' part, and when I asked Karen, she and Lesley only smirked and giggled together. I tried to pump Lesley for information when I got her on her own, but she pretended not to know what I was talking about. They are as thick as thieves these days, our daughters. Not that I feel left out. Anyway, it might be something else to quiz Howard about, re the vet's name.)

Must stop now, as I've been asked to take Cheryl Marie and little Nelson out for a walk so that Lesley and Karen can sleep late,

139

undisturbed. They went 'clubbing' last night, which apparently is less violent than it sounds. We used to call it 'going to a dance'. Their dances these days, though, don't seem to start until midnight, and go on until breakfast time. Thank heavens it hasn't always been like that—just think, if it had been, Cinderella would have turned into a pumpkin while still queuing to get into the ball, and Prince Charming wouldn't have looked twice. Unless he was a devout vegetarian, I suppose.

Oh dear, I am waxing lyrical. I've been missing my creative writing classes, and really must find time to go again. Perhaps I shall pen a poem in the park while I watch over my two little charges. Watch this space!!!

Much love,

Irene

Dear 'Nanny Spencer',

Thank you for the lovely card. Sabrina has pinned it to her wall. Her bedroom is still red, green and gold, which she tells me are 'roots'. I don't know what she means—I've never seen a parsnip in those colours.

We send love, and some new clothes, for Nelson and Cheryl Marie. I'd like them to wear something from me, other than a made-over box pleat. The dungarees can be let down if Nelson continues to elongate. Aren't the baby trainers sweet? They are thirty pounds in the shops here, but Yasmin gets them by the caseload from one of her clients who is a footwear specialist. She lays her hands on all sorts of things since she has taken her night job.

You are certainly whole-heartedly embracing your role of head cook and nappy washer. It sounds to me as though your goodwill is being rather exploited. I can't speak for Lesley, but Karen is, and always will be, a taker. She can wind people round her little finger—or in some cases, other parts of

141

her anatomy. Presumably that's why it's on display when she goes 'clubbing'. In no time she'll be in another unsuitable liaison and—perish the thought—another type of 'club'. I hope she doesn't suppose she is going to walk into this flat, or indeed any other council accommodation, when she returns with Nelson. Tony Blair is very down on single mothers. Especially serial ones. I imagine she will be a candidate for compulsory sterilisation.

Do take up your writing again. Creative or not, you must have something to while away the long hours on your own. Of course you have the children, and I adore Sabrina, but there are times when I long for a grown-up conversation—classical music, Art, double glazing . . .

We have finished painting the rest of Mandela Court. It is now a tasteful terracotta and very peaceful—apart from the African drumming. There! No sooner do I mention it than it starts again! Must go and investigate . . .

Later:

Sabrina and I had the most marvellous evening in No. 4, learning the female courting rituals of the Astarte tribe. Sara, my neighbour, is a Princess from it. The drum rhythms are compulsive. Everyone, from kids to pensioners, was gyrating madly. Apparently, in Africa, age is no handicap. Felt like a girl again! I could teach Karen and Lesley something about dancing. And courting. Next week we are having a session with the male members.

Must finish. Exhausted.

A bosom bounce and a hip wobble,

Vee

Dear Howard,

Karen has given your nephew a string of names longer than royalty. For everyday purposes, he will be known as 'Nelson'. I suppose a christening is out of the question, but do drop her a line.

Just remind me, was that nice vet called St John?

Mumsie xx

St Urban
Melbourne
Australia

Dear Vera,

In Deepest Sympathy
✝

Excuse the inappropriate card—it was all I had in my stationery box until I can find time to go out to the shops again, and I've used up all my notepaper in the penning of poems—one enc. for your perusal—thanks for encouraging me back to so pleasant a pastime. Lesley and Karen have gone up to Queensland for a week to lie down on the beach. Not that I feel left out. They are both suffering from exhaustion, apparently.

A big 'thank-you' from Cheryl Marie and Nelson for their new clothes. Yes, the pair of baby 'trainers' are very sweet, and after a good scrubbing I was able to clean off the rather nasty staining that was inside the left one. As you'll see from the enc. photos, Nelson has already grown in length since you last saw his picture, so until I find time to let his dungarees down, he is wearing them at the fashionable 'pedal-pusher' length.

More soon. Any news from Howard about the vet?

Much love from your poet pal,

Irene

PS Are 'blue bags' still available in England, do you know? Even when I boil them, the nappies are coming out a rather beige colour, which would certainly never have got past my mother's high standards. If you find any, please send them and I will reimburse.

Britannia—An Ode

by
Irene Spencer

O England,
You are so far away.
I wish that I could visit you,
If only for a day.

But I am needed here, my dear,
To watch o'er two of your babes.
To keep them safe and sound for you
Across the briny waves.

If I was there (or you were here),
I'd worship at your feet.
I'd wave at smiling bobbies and
I'd keep my garden neat.

I'd polish my silver tea set,
I'd wolf my fish and chips,
Your name, and praise accordingly,
Would never be off my lips.

O England,
You are the best there is,
How could I have forgot?
But I am here, and you are there,
And my heart aches quite a lot.

Dear Irene,

I'm really worried about you. Perhaps it is 'Poetic Licence', but you are euphemising an England which hasn't existed since the 1950s! It's clear you are very homesick. By the way, I've looked everywhere for Dolly Blues, as they used to be called, but like so much else, they haven't survived the onslaught of 'modernisation'. Are you, perhaps, feeding Nelson too much spinach? I recall my mother used to complain about the colour of tripe, which, as cows eat grass, was, in its natural state, green. I believe she used to soak it in bleach before putting it on my father's plate with gravy and onions. I don't think she ever used Dolly Blue. But that, as I was saying, was in the old days. I haven't seen tripe for sale for years. Makes one wonder, with all these new-fangled farming methods, whether cows still have stomachs.

I've spent sleepless hours (to be honest, not too many—I've been happily buggered after the African dance classes) thinking of you penning your verses in the lonely night. I'm

148

sure with two children to look after, you don't get the time, except in the wee small hours. Be wary—that's the time temptation strikes. We don't want you back in the funny farm.

Surely it's you who should be taking the holiday? Why don't you come home for one? You are welcome to stay here and share the joys of Mandela Court. We now have lots of African carvings and rugs and some wonderfully erotic tropical plants (the central heating is *very* effective). I can put Sabrina on the African reed 'futon' and you can have her room—as long as the colours don't bring on your migraine. It will only be for a short time, of course—I realise you are indispensable in St Urban.

Do reply soon, dear. Preferably not in the ode form.

All our love,

Vee and Sabrina

PS Are you allergic to dogs?

Darling Mumsie,

It's funny you should mention St John. *He's* been asking about the family. Well, about Karen to be specific. Waxing lyrical about their shared moments over entrails, in the sheep shed. Told the dear boy about the new addition and he got quite excited. Says he can't wait to see Nelson. I've sent Karen a gorgeous baby boiler-suit that Antony made out of sheepskin, and I've asked her for some photographs.

Is she coming home? Antony would adore a baby—you know how broody he gets. Besides, we miss Karen for the milking (the sheep, I mean!).

Your loving son,

Howie

Dear Vee,

You will *never* guess what's happened now, never ever in a million years. I'm reeling from the shock. I know I've been busy, but I can't believe I've been so blind! Lesley is marrying her boss!!!! Or at least, she intends to, once he's got a divorce from the very angry lady who called round to see me while Lesley and Karen were in Queensland. It turns out my daughter has been having an affair with the lady's husband for a year! Apparently 'Brian'—for that is his nomenclature—was in Queensland with them—his wife had him followed by a private detective.

You may think this shocking enough, but there's more. When Lesley got back from her holiday, I confronted her with my new and terrible knowledge, and begged her, in the name of decency, to leave the poor woman's husband alone. 'No, Mum,' she says, as bold as brass, 'it's too late for that.' When I continued to press my point, she suddenly got very angry and pointed at her stomach, and screamed 'I'm up the spout, you blind old bat, and it's his!' Vee—I'm going to be a granny again, in five

151

months' time! Then, without another word, she and Karen went out 'clubbing'—they said Lesley needed to taste her freedom as much as possible before she was 'lumbered' again with another baby.

Vera, I hope you are sitting down, because there's even more. No sooner had I sat down with a small sherry to digest this news than there was a knock at the door, and when I went to answer it, a blonde man with a suitcase and extraordinarily long legs bounced into the house and dashed past me, shouting, 'Where is he? Where's my baby boy?' Naturally, thinking this was 'Brian', and knowing now from the Damon experience that a lot of men are very naïve about making babies, I told him it was still in Lesley's tummy, where it would be staying for some long time yet, and he'd just have to wait. I knew I'd made a mistake when he asked me who the hell Lesley was, but I'd no idea how much of a mistake until he suddenly pulled himself together, apologised very nicely, said he was sorry then, perhaps he'd got the wrong house—he was looking for a Karen and Nelson Small—it was St John the Vet, come all the way from Great Shagthorne!!

As I write, in the wee small hours, Lesley is canoodling in her bedroom with 'Brian', Karen is curled up with St John in what used to be my room, and I am folded up on the sofa in the nursery with Cheryl Marie and Nelson. Not that I feel left out.

152

Heaven knows what tomorrow will bring! I'm wrung out and exhausted. If this is 'modernisation' and a taste of the new Minellium, please show me the way back to the 1950s immediately, Dolly Blues, bleached tripe and all! I'm too distressed even to write a poem.

Yours, shocked to the core,

Irene

PS I said a *small* sherry, Vera, just in case you're about to make silly and wild accusations again. Just remember—you're the one who said 'I am an alcoholic', not me.

Dearest darling Mumsie,

It's Horrorsville here—total chaos. St John, the vet, just took off in the middle of the insemination season, saying his own offspring was more important. If you ask me, he's been a bit too free with his services. The sheep are wandering around, bleating madly. So is Antony. He can't manage to impregnate them on his own, and he knows I faint at the sight of a syringe. He gets terribly cross with me, but, as I say, at least it ensures I'll never become a drug addict.

You absolutely must persuade them to come back. St John is indispensable, even if he is usually out of it on animal tranqs. That's why we're so late with the sheep—it took us months to drag him from his hovel. But he's the only vet we'll ever get around here. We'll even put up with Karen for his sake. And of course, we'd welcome the baby. There's a pair of fabby sheep-skin boots waiting, and Antony's already started casting the Runes for his future. He definitely sees him as a 'sheep' person, though I've pointed out he isn't an

Aries—thank goodness.

Please, please, do what you can. They can't be meaning to bring Nelson up with that frightful accent!

Your loving son,

Howie

Flat 2
19–23 Mandela Court
Thrush Grove
Vicker-upon-St Agnes

My dear Irene,

It never rains but it pours! Both of our daughters with new men and new babies! Let's hope it's wedding bells all round—and I don't care if that does make me sound old-fashioned!

You must come home immediately. Bring Cheryl Marie if necessary. I doubt Lesley will mind. Brian certainly won't. In my experience, men are a bit odd about adopting other males' children. There's plenty of room at Mandela Court. And I can assure you, you won't feel left out. This is a thriving, multi-national community—even Australians are welcome.

What are Karen's and St John's plans, do you know? I'm sure Lesley will want her 'space' back, now she has 'Brian'. No matter how bonded she and Karen have become, men always take precedence over female friendship. Please convey my good wishes to Karen and St John, and tell them that there's a home for their new family-to-be in Great Shagthorne.

Let me know your thoughts, and meanwhile

I'll have a word with the social worker, Ms Clinch, about housing. I'm sure our granddaughters would get on like a house on fire—not one of Ms Clinch's, of course! They are of an age, after all. It would give us a little respite too. Much as I love her, Sabrina runs me off my feet—I never expected to be looking after a small child again at my age. If I complain to my new neighbour, Princess Sara of the Astarte, she just laughs. She has six children and twenty-four grandchildren. They are in and out of her flat all the time. I've no idea how many actually live there.

You would love our jolly, neighbourly evenings—photos enc. That's me in the African turban. Will finish, as I must go and sweep up the beer cans in the court. We have a Residents' Rota, but it seems to fall mostly to Sara and me. We have to keep a clean front, in case of an unexpected raid by 'Environmental'. At least you wouldn't be drinking alone if you moved here. And whatever you say, one 'small' sherry tends to lead to another.

Write soon,

All our love,

Vee

Dear Vera,

Naturally we in St Urban are so relieved that you have taken time out of your busy schedule of going to neighbouring royalty's parties and clearing up your empty beer cans, to find time to organise all our lives, including where we will live and with whom.

Let me tell you that my initial reaction was 'How dare she?!!!' and, 'Who does she think she is?!!!', but after sitting for some quiet reflection in the Botanical Garden I have managed to get some perspective (without recourse to maryjuana tea, I might add, before you start thinking of referring me to Drugs Counselling) and tried to see it from your point of view, distorted and erroniatious as that might be.

Obviously, as you mention it in every letter now, you have a drink problem, and this you must admit to before you will make any headway at all with combating your desire to be needed and to be in control of everything and everyone, even those of us on the other side of the world. Think about it—if one small sherry leads to another for you, then you must stop having the small sherry. It may be hard at first, but you know it makes sense.

Gradually, as the alcohol fumes clear from your brain, you will start remembering important things, like the fact that I have my own perfectly lovely home to go to back in England, at 42 The Limes, Hethergreen. Have you forgotten so soon that you stayed with me there on the occasion of Bill Snapes's funeral (our ex-lover, if you're having trouble remembering)? But then again, I expect you have, since you were so drunk and incapable at the wake afterwards that you fell on to his widow's floral arrangements and a male member of the funeral party. Similarly, you have obviously also forgotten that the reason I left my beautiful home so suddenly to visit Australia in the first place was that you had sent Damon over to assassinate me and to destroy my flower beds.

The next revelation you might have is that Sabrina is your daughter Karen's child, not yours, and that she has left her with you to look after her until her return, which is imminent. After that, it might just dawn on you that St John, being a successful veterinarian surgeon, has his own wonderful house with grounds in neighbouring Little Shagthorne, so he does not need to be found digs in Great Shagthorne, presumably with your son Howard. You can't, of course, be expected to know that he has done Karen the honour of asking for her hand in marriage, and that she has accepted—invitation enc. They have asked me to mastermind the catering at the reception, which challenge I shall be delighted to rise to, and with which, if you care to, you are most welcome to assist.

Karen, St John, Nelson and myself are all flying back to England in a few days. I will not be kidnapping little Cheryl Marie, as her place is with her mother and Brian—who, incidentally, is besotted with her, and who can't wait to adopt her, as soon as his divorce comes through and he is free to marry again, since his previous marriage was unhappily childless. In the meantime, he will move in with Lesley to take care of her and his unborn child, as is proper in these modern circumstances.

The next time you hear from me I will be in England, by which time, I hope, you will be feeling better. It will be a relief for you to know that Karen will be moving in with St John immediately on their arrival, and will be taking little Sabrina to live with them, so you will soon have that respite from child-care duties that you were longing for in your last.

All good wishes for your speedy return to 'normal', whatever you remember that as being.

Irene

160

Irene,

Since you have opted to completely—and in my opinion, wilfully—misunderstand the helpful suggestions I made, with only goodwill and loving friendship in mind, I have decided that all future communication will be through my solicitor. You will be hearing from her shortly. I am considering filing charges against you in a civil court for slander and intentional theft of my daughter Karen's affections. I don't imagine, with your recent record of crazed behaviour, you will have a leg to stand on. Not that you do often anyway, what with your alcohol problem.

I have also informed our social worker, Ms Clinch, of Karen's intentions towards Sabrina, and all I can say is if her frowns and expletives are anything to go by, it will be over her dead body. Social services do not look kindly on women who abandon their children, particularly if they wish to reinstall them in unsuitable accommodation. You may like to know, as indeed might Karen, that according to my son Howard, St John's 'wonderful house

161

with grounds' consists of a bothy surrounded by a nettle patch, and that he narrowly escaped being struck off the veterinary register for over-use of animal tranquillisers. I don't give a crying baby much of a chance in that household!

As for you, you will find yourself once again in your pokey flat, home alone, except for a bottle. I wish I could say I sympathised—it is awful to feel left out—but I'm afraid that's what you get for meddling.

Sabrina and I will be unable to attend Karen's nuptuals (invitation returned), as the date clashes with our Mandela Millennial Carnival. Sabrina is playing a steel drum on the float. As I have pointed out more than once, it is important for her to be in touch with her 'roots'. Ms Clinch is in full agreement.

Yours faithfully,

V. Small

PS Since you say you are returning within days, I shall send this to your English address to welcome you.

162

Ingot & Camel-Hyman (Solicitors)
Lion House
Palm Walk
Vicker-upon-St Agnes

Dear Mrs Spencer,

I have been instructed by my client, Mrs Vera Small, to inform you that she is considering legal action against you on two counts:

1. Slander: With no evidence whatsoever, you have repeatedly called her an alcoholic.

2. Malicious alienation of her daughter Karen's affections: Mrs Small has not heard from her daughter once in the many months she has been away, and nor has her granddaughter, Sabrina. Even an invitation to her impending wedding came second-hand.

Out of common decency, Mrs Small also asks me to warn you that you will find yourself out of pocket if you decide to cater the reception. She has no intention of paying, and her son, Howard, insists Ms Small's intended husband is virtually bankrupt.

We look forward to receiving your comments.

Yours sincerely,

Agabatha Adebayou
(LLB, Queen of the Astarte)

42 The Limes
Hethergreen

Dear Vera,

Thank you for the warm welcome home
from you and your 'solicitor'. You both may be
distressed to know that, instead of panicking at
the threats of legal action against me, I
undertook some research via the telephone
and through my local library. I feel strongly
that I must inform you that:

1. Astarte was a fertility goddess
    worshipped by the Phoenicians, and not
    an African tribe at all.

2. The Law Society have never heard of
    Agabatha Adebayou, and neither does
    she have a degree in law.

3. She is a member of the Ladies League
    of Basketball in Vicker-upon-St Agnes,
    hence the letters 'LLB.' after her name.

I do hope you have not paid her fees, as she
is absolutely bogus from start to finish. I
showed your letter to Karen and St John, and

they laughed and laughed. Apparently St John named his twelve-bedroom Georgian hunting lodge 'The Bothy' as a joke, which your humourless son, Howard, obviously didn't get—and why should he, since he has never been invited over? As for the animal tranquillisers, once, while wrestling with one of Howard and Antony's more aggressive rams, St John accidentally jabbed his own arm rather than the creature's bottom, inadvertently sedating himself for several hours.

Since you are so obviously upset about not being able to attend their wedding due to a prior engagement, Karen has moved the date forward to January 2000. She will be hand-delivering the invitation, I believe, at which point she will also be inviting you to live with them in the granny flat at 'The Bothy', so that you don't have to feel you are losing Sabrina.

All for now, as I must away to an emergency meeting of the Hethergreen Village Minellium Bus Shelter Fund Committee. I left them with a few simple chores while I was away in Australia and they have done nothing. With only a few weeks to go to the great event of the new Minellium, and nothing in Hethergreen so far to show for it, I have organised a Do-It-Ourselves Digging of the Foundations Event this morning.

I do hope this letter finds you feeling more like your old self. If so, let's start planning the menu for the New Year wedding. If not, please do not trouble yourself to reply.

Yours in memory of a long and trusty
friendship,

Irene

Dear Irene,

Well, here I am ensconned in the 'Granny' flat (though St John always jokes I look much too young to be one—what a tease that boy is!), and I must say they have bent over backwards to make it nice for me. St John, of course, is just a naturally kind and delightful person—as well as rich and good-looking. Quite the Prince Charming.

Karen, for once, seems to know how lucky she is (especially with feet her size), and is a completely changed person. She came to see me in Mandela Court of her own devolition and said, 'Mum, if only I'd realised years ago how much you needed and wanted my love, everything would have been quite different.' I was taken aback, I can tell you, particularly as it was a Voodoo evening and I had white paint and feathers all over my head and was up to my elbows in chicken blood.

I told Sara about your suspicions, by the way, and she roared with laughter. Agabatha, her niece, is studying law at night school, and it was only silly me supposing 'Astarte' was

168

African. In fact, Sara is a modern-day reincarnation of the Goddess, and the 'tribe' part are the others involved with her rites. I do miss them.

But it's lovely to have my family close, and I shall soon get used to seeing nothing but hills outside my window. Pushing Nelson's pram up them is the very devil!

Now, about the wedding. What do you think about 'Coq o' Vin' as the main course? (It's one of Sara's recipes.)

Vee

42 The Limes
Hethergreen

Dear Vera,

Brief note, haven't got long—the male members of the Committee put the Minellium Bus Shelter up last night, and it is down again this morning with the winds. I thought at the time as I watched them doing all that 'bonding' business with their cans of lager that men are so fond of, hours before the concrete mixer had even arrived, that if a thing is worth doing, it's worth doing yourself. I really don't know why I don't listen to myself more.

Glad you're happy being Mother-in-Law (pre-marriage) to Prince Charming, and that you have seen enough sense to be rescued from that cult—they are dangerous things. It starts all jolly and fun with feathers and white paint, and ends with poison in your orange juice and mass suicide pacts—I saw a documentary on television once, and believe you me it wasn't for the squeamish.

Now as to the wedding menu. I have been planning a Fork and Finger, not a sit-down do, so Coq o' Vin would be quite inappropriate. I thought you could make your old favourite, the Blue Cheese Quiche, but with one refinement—I've been experimenting with the

170

addition of chives, and it lifts it from the ordinary to the sublime. I think we should give your salmon mousse a miss though, given my upset tummy last time I had it at yours, but perhaps you could mastermind the salads?

So glad we are friends again. Let me know your thoughts on the above.

Much love,

Irene

PS. I think, all things considered, it would be wise to let St John do the tasting and ordering of the wine.

Dear Irene,

You certainly should listen to yourself more. Of all the rude, ungrateful, ignorant, bossy, self-opinionated, interfering . . . I could go on, but I haven't got a dictionary to hand. You'd better hold your tongue, or you'll find one of your 'Minellium' Committee putting poison in *your* orange juice. At the moment I'd be glad to supply it!

Later.
Have just been for a stiff walk up a mountain. Spoke to Jesus at the top and feel a lot better. If he could turn the other cheek for 2,000 years, I can manage till after the wedding— salad recipes enclosed.

Irene, do let's enter the Millenium as we mean to go on—with tolerance.

In love and friendship,

Vera